BETWEEN THE TREES

BY

AYN O'REILLY WALTERS

Grosvenor House
Publishing Limited

This book is published by
Grosvenor House Publishing Ltd
Link House
140 The Broadway, Tolworth, Surrey, KT6 7HT.
www.grosvenorhousepublishing.co.uk

This book is a work of fiction. Any resemblance to
people or events, past or present, is purely coincidental.

A CIP record for this book
is available from the British Library

ISBN 978-1-83975-828-7

For my wonderful family

PROLOGUE

A jewel of gold
the passage of time
in two hands
doth break the line.

PART 1 - 2013

PART I • 2014

CHAPTER 1

Isabel Pritchard was a regular twelve-year-old girl. She went to school and rather liked it. In the evenings, she did all of her homework, ate all of her dinner (well, most of it) and happily helped out with her chores around the house. On the other hand, her brother, William, was a moody sixteen-year-old who didn't want to spend any time with his sister. He preferred spending his evenings in his bedroom all by himself and only ventured out when dinner was ready. It was fair to say that Isabel and William didn't get along. However, one day would change all that. It was a day that would change their lives forever.

On that particular day, Isabel woke at seven o'clock in the morning. She opened her bleary eyes, sat up in bed, stretched out her arms and remembered today was school sports day. Getting dressed, the smell of breakfast floated down the hallway. It smelled good and she realised how hungry she was.

Isabel traipsed into the kitchen and sat at the small breakfast table. William didn't acknowledge her as he was too busy stuffing his face with pancakes topped with peanut butter.

"Oh, William!" cried Isabel as she scraped butter on her toast.

William, with his mouth full of food, looked up and replied, "Better than your sourdough. Sour-dough. Sums it up perfectly."

"You'll die of a heart attack with all the rubbish you eat."

"Why can't you just get along?" Mother asked as she stood at the sink pouring her second cup of coffee. "You only have each other so be nice. That's all I ask of you both."

Although William spent much of his time alone in his room, he was very intelligent. He began playing chess with his father at three and at eight would drag his mother to the local library and borrow all of the history books. He was fascinated with the world and its origins. While most of his friends played football on a Saturday morning, William preferred to read books on anatomy and medicine as he had aspirations of becoming a doctor after finishing school. He had his life mapped out. He would complete his medical degree at a top university and work in a prominent hospital in London. Isabel, however, wasn't so sure about her future. She loved animals and thought of becoming a vet. She still had plenty of time to decide. Right now, she just wanted to get through her final year of primary school.

"It's Daddy's birthday on Sunday," whispered Mother. Neither Isabel or William responded. They ate silently as Mother squeezed their hands then began clearing the breakfast dishes.

"Has it been four years already?" Isabel asked.

"Yes, four years, my darling," replied Mother.

"I miss him so much, Mum."

"We all do." Mother looked over at William, waiting for him to say something. Instead, he swiftly got up, said a quick 'bye' and was gone.

Since their father died, Mother had to take a second job to pay the school fees and make the house payments. No longer could they afford to go on holidays during the summer and school holidays didn't feel the same anymore. The house was empty when Isabel came home from school every afternoon and when William got home he would go straight to his room and stay there for most of the evening. Mother often arrived home after dark and it was up to Isabel and William to do their homework, prepare their dinner and get ready for bed.

When Isabel arrived at school that day, she made her way straight to class as sports day meant there were no lessons all day. The school bell rang and, soon enough, the corridors emptied out as children dashed into their classrooms. Jess was Isabel's best friend and they sat next to each other every day. "Hey, Isabel, want to come to my house after school on Friday? Mum said you can come for dinner."

"Sure. I'll ask Mum to pick me up on her way home from work which means we can watch telly 'til late."

"And skip our homework," giggled Jess.

On the way to the sports ground, the girls sat together on the bus and chatted about their upcoming school holidays. They decided to save as much pocket money as they possibly could to spend the lot on sweeties and crisps. Jess and Isabel had been best friends for three years, after Jess's family moved to London from a small village in Nottingham. It was in the corridor at school when they first met. Jess was lost and couldn't find her classroom. She walked from door to door, peering into each class, looking for a door labelled 'Class 3P'. The 'P' stood for Mrs Peterson. Isabel was on her way to Class 3P and seeing that Jess was lost, asked if she needed any help. When the girls realised they were in the same class, Isabel showed Jess to their classroom. They sat next to each other that morning and had done ever since.

Sports day dragged on for Isabel. She competed in the relay and 200-metre races and reluctantly participated in the shotput and discus events. It was a tiring day so she walked home slowly and wondered whether William would already be home. *It won't matter if he is*, she thought. *He'll just be in his room anyway and I'll be on my own again.* Realising it was getting late, Isabel decided to cut through Bishops Park to halve the journey time. Mother warned William and Isabel not to cut through the park but it was still daylight and Isabel could see the back of her house from the park entrance so she thought it would be okay and she presumed Mother wouldn't find out anyway.

Isabel picked up her pace and walked briskly through the big iron gates at the park entrance. Her thoughts had turned to the maths homework she had to finish that evening when, halfway through the park, she noticed a bright light that looked like it was coming from a tree. The closer she walked towards the tree, the brighter the light shone. It was an unusual light, not like the glow of the sun or a brightly lit torch but a myriad of colours: purple, pink, blue, gold. They all seemed to blend into each other creating colours she had never seen before. It looked magical and instantly drew her closer to the tree so she stepped away from the path and began walking towards the tree, completely unaware of any danger she might be getting herself into. The colours were mesmerising and she couldn't stop and return to the path. She didn't want to return to the path, she didn't want to go home, not yet, not until she knew why the tree was glowing. She stood at the base of the tree. Slowly she raised her hands, reached out and felt a warmth coming directly from the trunk. When her hands were almost touching the tree, she stopped. *What will happen if I touch this?* she thought. *Will I die? Will I get sick? Will nothing happen at all?* It was all so peculiar and the urge to understand why the tree was so warm overwhelmed her. "Do it," she whispered. She closed her eyes and suddenly the earth beneath her began to shake. Losing her balance, she felt dizzy and started to scream. All of a sudden, a gust of wind rushed up from under her feet and lifted her up into the air. She was only a few centimetres off the ground, yet she felt like she was flying high in the sky, way above the treetops.

Then suddenly everything stopped. The tree stopped glowing and she felt her feet back firmly on the ground. Everything was quiet again. Opening her eyes, she looked around and everything looked exactly the same. She looked up at the big old oak and wondered what had just happened. She felt frightened and ran away, looking for the path to take her home. Scrambling around, she realised it wasn't there. The path was gone! She became confused and ran as fast as she could to the big iron gates at the park entrance and when she ran through the gates, she got the shock of her life. Gone were the cars screeching around corners on cemented roads. Instead, horses and wagons clopped up and down the muddy street.

Bewildered, Isabel stared in amazement at the scene before her. Men walked slowly up and down the street in their top hats, black coats and knee-length boots, arm in arm with ladies in their colourful bonnets and big billowing dresses that dragged along the mud on the ground. The sound of everyday life could be heard by market stall owners selling fruit and vegetables at the end of the street. Little girls in old tattered clothes walked up and down the street selling bouquets of flowers from their baskets. "Please, sir, please buy my flowers," said a young girl to an older gentleman. She was probably the same age as Isabel. The young girl was clearly poor, for she was terribly skinny and her dirty blonde hair was long and knotted.

Isabel slowly peered down at her feet. Instead of the trainers she wore to school that day, her feet were tightly fitted in black boots, tied with laces, partially covered with a frilled petticoat. She was wearing a beige coloured dress with buttons from the waist all the way up to her neck. A crimson shawl was wrapped around her shoulders and she realised her clothes were similar to the very people she was observing.

On the pavement, she noticed a man selling newspapers. He wore an old pair of trousers with holes in the knees, worn shoes and no socks. A dark brown shirt hung over his big belly and his face was old and wrinkled. A pile of newspapers were stacked up against a shop window next to him, held together by pieces of string. The man started yelling, "Chronicle! Queen Victoria visits Great Exhibition." Unbeknown to Isabel, the year was 1851.

CHAPTER 2

Isabel gasped and started shaking. What was happening? *Am I in another world? I want to go home*, she thought. She turned around and ran back into the park, a place she was familiar with, the way home and a place that felt safe – at least safer than the world she had just seen. Upon seeing the oak tree, she ran faster, puffing and panting. She held out her arms and hugged it so hard that the palms of her hands slapped against the bark with a thud.

Slowly Isabel opened her eyes and looked around. She was at home, tucked up in her bed. Looking up, she saw a familiar face. It was Mother, sitting on the bed, holding her hand.

"Oh, darling, you're awake," she said quietly.

"Oh, Mum, what happened? Where's the girl with the flowers?"

"What girl?" Isabel sat up and looked around at her small bedroom. "Honey," said Mother, "you were late home from school so William and I went looking for you. We found you in the park lying under a big tree. You must have fainted or fallen asleep. Now lie down and rest and I'll bring your dinner."

As Mother stood up and walked towards the door, she hesitated, turned around at looked straight at Isabel. "And stay away from that park," she said sternly and walked out closing the door behind her.

That night Isabel had trouble sleeping. She woke several times wondering what on earth happened in the park. She just couldn't figure out why the man was selling newspapers about a queen who died over a hundred years ago. It must have been a bad dream. Next morning she dressed for school and joined William and Mother at the breakfast table but she couldn't eat. She was too confused to warrant an appetite.

"What happened to you yesterday?" William nudged Isabel with his elbow.

Before Isabel could reply, Mother interrupted. "Forget about it, kids, nothing happened, Isabel just fainted. Probably a bit unwell," she said, taking a bite of her toast.

"Yeah, unwell alright," laughed William. Isabel gave him a cold stare.

"Okay, kids, that's enough," Mother said sternly. "I'm off to work." She lent over the table and gave Isabel a quick cuddle and kissed William on the forehead. Then she was gone.

Isabel waited for the front door to close then almost burst out William's name. "William! Something weird happened in the park. I didn't faint. I think I went into another time or place." Isabel spent the next ten minutes describing the lights surrounding the big oak tree and what had happened when she touched it. Realising William was having trouble believing her, she said, "Fine, I'll show you myself. We'll go to the park after school and you can see for yourself".

"Sure," replied William. "This will be a hoot. See you in the park after school."

Four o'clock came and Isabel waited patiently for William at the park entrance. All day she had been thinking about what might happen that afternoon and whether they would see the same strange events as the previous day. William eventually showed up and they entered the park together. "All right, where's this magic tree then," William asked. "You'd better hurry up, I've got an essay due tomorrow."

"Just up ahead. It's the big one right there." Isabel pointed to the big oak.

Unlike the bigger parks in London, such as Hyde Park, Bishops Park was quite small. The main path lead from the front entrance past the big oak tree towards a small pond. On the other side of the pond was a small cottage in which the park caretaker lived. He was a grumpy old man called Mr Brown. Every morning, Mr Brown would hop into his buggy and drive around the park collecting the rubbish that people left behind and at eight o'clock every night he would stand at the park entrance with his big set of keys dangling on a chain, waiting to close the park for the night. He hated animals and didn't allow them into the park. As a result, not many people ventured into the park and this was how he liked it. It was more or less used as a shortcut for people to get from Windermere Road, where Isabel lived, to the main street where all of the shops were.

As they drew nearer the tree, Isabel noticed there was no light coming from the tree. It seemed odd, but what wasn't odd about this event? In any case, she told William to slap the trunk and hold his hands there. She did the same and closed her eyes. Nothing happened. The earth didn't shake. The only sound she heard was William laughing. "Gee, sis, that *was* funny."

"It happened, it really did. Just the way I told you this morning." Isabel began crying.

"Aah, don't worry about it, sis, let's go home. I won't tell anyone about your silly dream."

"It wasn't a dream, I swear. Really, William, you must believe me."

William collected their school bags from the ground and threw them over his shoulder. "Come on, we've got homework to do."

Walking home, Isabel couldn't understand why the tree didn't shake or emit colours or why she didn't feel the warmth emanating from it. Perhaps it was because William was there, maybe the magic only worked if Isabel was alone. Perhaps it was the wrong time of day, or week. Isabel felt confused and foolish. Foolish for bringing William to the tree. Now he would think she was stupid and, knowing William, he would probably tease her about this for the rest of her life.

As they walked along the cobbled path past Mr Brown's house Isabel glanced to her left and there it was again! The same lights glowing yet from a different tree. She felt a warm sensation and passing the tree she saw the colours all blending into each other, just like yesterday. Isabel gently tugged William's jacket and whispered, "Look over there, do you see it?"

William looked over and stopped in his tracks. He was in utter shock. They both stared at the elm, which was much smaller than the oak tree. William began slowly walking towards the tree. Isabel followed. When they reached the tree, they both looked at each other and in silence raised their hands and touched the tree together. Once again, the ground started shaking and William yelled out as loud as his lungs would allow.

"William!" screamed Isabel.

All of a sudden, the ground stopped shaking and the colours disappeared. The children stood there in silence. The park was quiet again. Turning to Isabel, William said, "What just happened?"

"This is it!" squealed Isabel. "This is what I was telling you about. We need to get out of the park to see the horses and wagons and the little girl selling flowers. This way." Isabel grabbed her brother's hand and raced back towards the park entrance.

"Oh my Gosh! Look at all this!" William gasped when they stepped into the street. This time, however, not a horse or wagon was in sight. Colourful bunting hung from all of the shop windows. Hundreds of people filled the streets dancing, cheering and waving Union Jack flags. Music could be heard bellowing out of gramophones and children cheekily hung out of the windows of old cars as they drove around the streets.

"You two, over there!" yelled a young man. "Don't look so glum, why it's the greatest day on earth! Come on over and dance with us." The young man was dressed in green combat trousers and jacket with a matching cap. A tan leather belt went all the way around his waist and his matching shoes were shiny and clean, just like the row of medals perched on the pocket of his jacket.

Now it was William's turn to look around in bewilderment. "Is this for real?"

"You better believe it," replied Isabel. "I knew I wasn't going mad."

"I think we're both going mad," said William. "Look at us." They were wearing different clothing. William had on a brown pair of corduroy shorts, white shirt and a yellow knitted sleeveless vest, while Isabel was wearing a pair of black shoes, short white socks, green pleated tunic and a blue wool cardigan.

"Oh, I forgot to mention that," Isabel chuckled.

"We must be in another time."

"Yes! And when we enter that time, we are wearing those clothes," replied Isabel. "Let's find out what year it is then."

"No need," William said as he gazed at the scene before him. It's the end of the war. It must be VE Day, which means we're in 1945."

"What do we do now?" asked Isabel. "I don't want to go back home yet."

"Nor do I. Let's explore." The children stepped into the street and disappeared amongst the crowd.

Walking along the main street, Isabel and William noticed that their local computer store was now an ice cream parlour. Children sat at the window licking ice creams and scooping up their sundaes with big spoons. Isabel watched a little boy licking chocolate ice cream from his hand as it trickled all the way down to his elbow. The next shop, which used to be a health food store, was now a pharmacy. A lady stood near the front window picking up small glass bottles from a shelf and a bell on top of the door rang every time someone entered. Everything was different, all of the shops were different, even the cars were different. At the end of the street, where a roundabout would normally have been, was a grassy embankment. People of all ages sat there on rugs drinking and eating. Children played and babies were pushed around by their mothers in silver prams with big wheels, rocking gently to and fro.

The streets were packed with people and the ground was covered with confetti and Union Jack flags. Everybody looked elated. As Isabel and William walked through the streets, they looked around in sheer amazement. "I just can't believe it," William said.

"Do you think the trees are magic?" asked Isabel.

"They must be."

"But it's strange to think that yesterday there were horses and wagons. And I heard a man yelling something about Queen Victoria."

"Queen Victoria?" William stopped and firmly held Isabel's shoulder. "You must have been in the 1800s then. But today we're in 1945. I have no idea why we're in a different century."

"We need to find out," Isabel said. "It *must* have something to do with the trees."

"I guess we could ask Mr Brown about their history."

"Yep," said Isabel excitedly. "Let's ask Mr Brown, he might know something about the two trees we travelled through."

As William looked around at all the amazing sights in 1945, he noticed it was getting dark. "All right we'd better be getting home now, it's getting late."

"Do you think we should tell Mother?"

"Oh gosh, no," replied William. "She'll completely freak out. Let's keep this to ourselves until we find out what on earth is going on here."

The children made their way back to the park and together placed their hands on the elm. Shortly afterwards they were back in the present day for they could see Mr Brown with his big chain of keys walking towards the front gate of the park. They slipped out through the back gate and returned home. As they walked through their front door, Mother's car pulled up in the driveway. *That was a close one*, the children thought.

CHAPTER 3

The following morning, at breakfast, the children had something to smile about. They sat at the table, William chowing down his pancakes and peanut butter and Isabel with her sourdough and marmite. Only this time, they weren't arguing. There were no sarcastic remarks directed at each other. Instead, they sat happily grinning like Cheshire cats. Mother almost dropped her cup of coffee when she observed William open the fridge and pour two glasses of milk, one for Isabel and one for himself.

"Alright," Mother said. "What's going on?"

"Whatever do you mean?" Isabel asked, sarcastically smirking at William.

"Well, for one, William pouring a glass of milk for his little sister is a first and I've not witnessed any bickering between the two of you either."

"I guess you could say I now have *time* for my little sister," replied William as they both burst out laughing.

Mother shook her head and rolled her eyes then began stacking the dishes in the sink. She was grateful for the peace and wondered whether her children might finally start getting along now. Maybe it just took some time after their father died for things to get back to normal. Well, as normal as life could be without him.

As soon as Mother left for work, Isabel and William decided to undertake a little detective work surrounding the magic trees in the park. They discussed how they should approach Mr Brown, being such a grump and all, and what questions they would ask him. They realised it was best not to tell him about the trees taking them back in time, after all, who would possibly believe them? They would be laughed at or thought of as just little children playing a silly joke. So they decided to pretend they were doing a school project about their local park and the history of the trees within it.

Mother working long hours during the week was hard on the children, however, it did have its advantages as they had time to visit Mr Brown after school before she came home. During the day, Mother worked as a nurse at the local hospital and in the evenings she worked at a doctors surgery so the children had more than enough time to do their homework and have some time to themselves before bed. It was decided they would go and see Mr Brown immediately after school, well before he closed the park. They met at the entrance to the park once again and excitedly walked along the path towards the cobbled stones. William felt nervous and wondered what questions to ask, while Isabel felt excited and thought about sitting down with Mr Brown having a lovely chat over tea and scones.

When they approached the house it was much larger than it looked from the other side of the pond. The small fence around the perimeter of the house was made of wire with weeds sprouting from wooden posts that held the gate in place. The grass in the small front garden was overgrown and a narrow brick path led to three steps on the front porch. Torn curtains hung from two big windows on either side of the front door. The house was so old it looked as though it was about to fall down. On the porch sat an old rocking chair with worn cushions on the seat. A big black cat had made the chair its home and, curled up on the cushions, didn't notice the children as they walked up the three steps and stood at the front door. It was only 4.30 in the afternoon yet it felt much later. William nervously knocked on the door and they waited.

"What is it?" bellowed a voice from inside. "What do you want?"

William's voice trembled. "I'm... Er... William Pritchard and I'm doing a school project on your park..."

"Go away," yelled the voice.

"Please... Mr Brown?" William paused. "We love the park and everyone thinks you've done an amazing job looking after it, and, well…" Suddenly footsteps approached and the door opened. Mr Brown stood at the threshold and looked the children up and down. He was an odd looking man, not much taller than William. He had a big nose, way too big for his little face, with red cheeks, small brown eyes and big bushy eyebrows. Isabel thought he must be a hundred years old to have eyebrows that long. He was almost completely bald and wore a grey knitted jumper with holes at the elbows and brown corduroy trousers. He stood there, chewing the remains of his meal as he wiped his hands on the front of his jumper.

"Er, as I was saying, I'm William and this is my sister, Isabel." William motioned to Isabel who was actually starting to feel a little afraid of Mr Brown. Everybody knew he was grumpy but Isabel sensed there was something more sinister to the old caretaker.

William began explaining that he was researching the history of the park and, before he could finish his sentence, Mr Brown took a step back into the house and said in a menacing voice, "There is no 'istory 'ere. The park ain't got no 'istory and you shouldn't be pokin' yer nose around where it don't belong." With that, he slammed the door shut. The frightened children quickly turned around, ran down the path through the rickety gate and stopped when they reached the pond, well clear of the old house.

"That went well," said William, puffing.

"There's something not right about him, I think he knows something."

"What do you mean, Izzy?"

"Just the way he spoke. He became so angry when you mentioned the word 'research'. It was like he didn't want us to find anything out at all."

"You're right. I got that impression too. Well, it looks like we shall have to go it alone then."

After a few moments, when the children caught their breaths, Isabel said, "William, don't you think it's strange that both Mother and Mr Brown are so weird about anything to do with the park? I mean, Mother won't even let us near it and Mr Brown won't even talk about it. Don't you think that's odd?"

"Perhaps. Maybe Mother just doesn't like us walking through the park for safety reasons. Maybe she wants to keep us away from Mr Brown because he's a really nasty person. I guess that's reason enough. He scared the wits out of me today."

"Me too."

"Ha! I've got it. We'll start at the library. Surely they'll have some historical facts about the park." William looked at his watch. It was a quarter to five. "Let's see if the library is open. Come on, we can make it if we run."

The children ran through the park and headed down the main street. Puffing and panting, they arrived at the library just after 5 o'clock. The glass door of the old brick building slid open and they entered. Rows of books and journals adorned tall shelves on either side of the walls and straight ahead sat a big old desk with stacks of books piled on top of it. Two small chains held a sign at the front of the desk with the words 'Reception' in big black letters.

"Over there," said William as he led the way to the front desk.

When they reached the desk a young woman popped out from behind a shelf. "Can I help you?" she asked.

"Oh, yes please. We are wondering whether you have any history books on Bishops Park. It's for a school project and any information would greatly help."

"Well," said the young woman, "normally I wouldn't do this but since you put it so politely and it's almost closing time, pop round to my side and we'll see what we can find on the computer."

The trio huddled close together watching the screen as the woman typed away on the keyboard. "Bishops Park," she muttered. "Hmm, let's see. Oh! Here we are. All of the village newspapers were recently added to our computer system so if you look right here, you can see an index of every newspaper dating back to 1803. It appears that the 10th December of that year is the first issue of *The Finlay Gazette.*" The children excitedly looked at each other. "So I'll leave you to it and be back a bit later on. We close at 6pm sharp."

"Thank you," they said together as the young lady wandered off with a handful of books.

"Okay, Izzy, all we need to do is type in 'Bishops Park' and see what comes up." After a few seconds, a headline on the front page of *The Finlay Gazette,* titled, 'WINDERMERE WETLANDS TO BECOME TOWN'S NEW PARK' popped up. It was dated 6 February 1822. "Looks like the park was built after 1822," whispered William. "Although I can't find anything written about the oak tree. Now, you travelled to the 1800s, didn't you? I mean, that newspaper man was selling papers about Queen Victoria. We need to find out what year that was. What exactly did he say?"

"He said something about an exhibition. That's it! Queen Victoria attends the Great Exhibition."

"Well done, Isabel. So if I type in 'Queen Victoria Great Exhibition' let's see what comes up." The children waited while the computer scanned through hundreds of newspaper headings.

"There!" said Isabel. "Stop! It's that exact same newspaper the old man was selling." It was dated 7 May 1851.

"Gee whiz. Do you know what this could mean, Isabel? If the oak tree in the park is where you took your first journey, it might very well have been planted in 1851."

"Of course. And when we both went to 1945, it was through another tree. I bet that tree was planted in 1945."

Standing at the reception desk, the children looked at each other in bewilderment. They had been living right next door to a magical park all their lives and had no idea until now. They wondered why they were able to travel and whether any other people were able to travel too. What if somebody else touched the trees? Would they also travel in time?

The young librarian returned to her desk and told the children it was almost closing time. Realising they hadn't even thought about their homework, the children decided to catch the bus home so they could get their chores finished before Mother arrived home. They needed everything to look as normal as possible in order not to arouse suspicion. If Mother knew they had been in the park she would be most upset and might even ground them and that would be disastrous, just as they were finding out about the magic trees.

On the bus, William and Isabel decided they would return to the oak tree and go back to 1851 where Isabel's adventure began. For every question they had there were a hundred more. The only way they could be safe while they travelled, however, would require money, for they didn't know how long they would be gone. They needed money for food and somewhere to sleep, if necessary. The children didn't do any homework that evening. Instead they stayed up most of the night sitting on William's bed, discussing how they would get by financially in 1851, how they would buy food and where they would stay. Realising that currency had changed over the years, today's currency would be worthless. They may as well have tried to buy food with scraps of newspapers!

If they couldn't take money they would take the next best thing, something valuable they could sell once they were back in the nineteenth century. William had several trophies, however, being made of brass, they wouldn't fetch much, if anything, at all. He figured it was worth a try so they bundled up the trophies and anything else they could find in their bedrooms that might be worth selling. They eventually climbed into their beds and fell into a deep sleep. Waking the next morning, they were ready to visit the Great Exhibition of 1851.

CHAPTER 4

After discussing when to travel back, William figured the sooner the better, so they decided the following Monday after school would be the best time to resume their adventure through the oak tree. The week went ever so slowly and when Monday finally arrived, they finished school and met at the entrance of Bishops Park. As they walked briskly over to the oak tree, they felt excited, apprehensive, and a little terrified.

"Let's do this," said William and together they placed their hands upon the big oak tree once again. The children felt the dizzy sensation with the earth beneath them shaking. "Hold on!" shouted William. Then silence. Standing still in the park, they knew they had travelled back as Isabel was wearing the same black boots, buttoned up dress and crimson shawl she had worn on her first visit. William wore knickerbockers with a cream shirt tucked into them and a black waistcoat. "Don't I look the part?" he chuckled as he inspected his new clothing. Isabel spun around, the frills at the bottom of her dress blowing upward in the wind.

The children headed towards the park exit and walked down the embankment alongside the Thames towards Westminster Abbey. Life was quite different for the inhabitants of London in the 1800s. London's new sewerage system hadn't been completed so all of the waste from the city ended up in the River Thames. And it stank! Not being used to such living conditions, the children couldn't bear the smell and decided to walk in the opposite direction, through St James's Park, until they reached Buckingham Palace. How different it looked. There were no big black iron gates surrounding the palace, in fact there were no gates at all. It looked rather like a big house with grass and trees. People walked past, horses trotted back and forth and everybody went along as though it was just an ordinary house, albeit a very big one. You could walk right up to the front of the building and touch it! Isabel thought it was incredible how the public could get within such proximity to Queen Victoria.

The children kept walking until they reached Hyde Park whereupon they stopped to see an enormous structure made entirely of glass. It was so big that it was impossible to miss. "It's the Great Exhibition!" William exclaimed. "This is it!" They walked over towards the glass building. As they drew nearer, the building became bigger and bigger until they were standing in front of a big glass dome near the entrance. To the left and right, the glass structure seemed endless. It was several stories tall with a semicircular roof. It was built of nothing but glass.

Hundreds of horses and carriages pulled up as coachmen jumped down from their seats to open carriage doors for ladies dressed in big billowing crinolines and gentlemen in top hats wearing long tails that hung down the bottom of their suit jackets. People lined up as far as the eye could see. Children excitedly held hands with their mothers as they waited in the queue to enter the most magnificent exhibition in the history of England.

At the entrance, the children noticed a sign on a glass panel. It read:

Entry – £2 for gentleman, £1 for ladies. The Great Exhibition will be open to the general public on 24th May at one shilling each.

"William, we don't have any money, remember?" said Isabel.

"I have a plan. Follow me and don't say anything." William led Isabel away from the main entrance and walked alongside the building until they came to a goods entrance where men carried items and boxes into the building. Seeing a stack of empty boxes on a wagon, William picked up two smaller ones and handed one to Isabel. They followed a group of workers into the building and hid the boxes behind a plant adjacent to the door.

The inside of the building was dazzling. The dome-shaped roof was held together with big panes of glass as the gleaming sun that shone through lit up the whole building. As the children walked through the building, rows of exhibits were on display with merchants showcasing everything from furs and ivory, to bicycles and rubber tubes. On the left was a section with printing presses, textile machines and a steam engine machine. There must have been every type of invention in the world under one roof. Flags from all over the world filled the rooms with colour. It was a reminder of the influence and importance of the British Empire during the period. It was Britain's time to shine above almost every other country in the world and every other country in the world was there. Palm trees filled the aisles and throngs of people chatted excitedly while others just stood looking around, amazed.

Towards the middle of the building a huge fountain was clearly the showcase of the Great Exhibition. It too was made of glass and had several towers spurting water, which trickled all the way down to the bottom. An enormous tree, lush with green leaves, almost reached the top of the dome, providing a focal point for people to meet. Groups of gentlemen stood together smoking cigars whilst admiring the surroundings, their wives fanning themselves with their elegant hands in white lace gloves.

"What is this place?" asked Isabel.

"It's the world's biggest exhibition. I read about this at the library one day. Prince Albert was the brains behind it. Apparently all the profits went into building the Natural History Museum as well as the Science Museum and many other museums in Kensington. You've been to most of them."

"Unbelievable."

"Yep," said William. "It's called the Crystal Palace and unfortunately it's destroyed by fire sometime in the future, although nobody knows that yet!"

The children continued walking around the exhibits, taking in all the sights and new inventions. William stopped to listen to a man and woman chatting to one another at a nearby stall. The man was dressed just as a gentleman would in a fine suit and crisp white shirt. He had curly black hair, slightly balding on top, and a moustache and goatee. The conversation pricked William's ears and he stopped to listen.

"Why, no, my dear," said the man. "It's simply not humane to expect children of such a young age to work those hours."

"Indeed," agreed the woman. "However, longer hours would mean greater productivity among the workhouses."

"Hey, Izzy," screeched William. "That's Charles Dickens!"

"No way," she replied.

"He's talking about conditions in the workhouses. He lobbied for better working conditions for everyone, especially children."

"He sounds like a great man," said Isabel.

Walking past the India exhibit, the children saw the largest diamond in the world, the Koh-i-noor, meaning 'mountain of light'. The 105-carat diamond was acquired by Britain and formed part of Queen Victoria's Crown Jewels. It was a spectacular sight.

Many famous people visited the exhibition, most of whom Isabel and William did not recognise. Famous writers, such as Charlotte Bronte and Lewis Carroll, were there. Charles Darwin also visited the Great Exhibition. A military band played music in the background when Queen Victoria and Prince Albert arrived shortly afterwards. Outside, the crowd cheered and waved their handkerchiefs high in the air at the royal procession. It was clear that the Victorians adored their queen. As the Queen made her way inside, she was greeted by members of her court, government ministers and a young man named Joseph Paxton, who was of no importance, having been a gardener, until he designed the magnificent structure. He was the toast of the exhibition, along with Prince Albert, who worked tirelessly to have the exhibition built and ready for its opening day on 1 May 1851. The Queen looked so proud standing next to her husband and she beamed with delight whenever he spoke. They chatted to the Duke of Wellington and Lord Anglesey, the unsung heroes of the Battle of Waterloo, who, now in their eighties, walked arm in arm together. It was a lovely sight for the Queen to see as Anglesey had previously fallen foul of Wellington's favour. Later the Queen would make a note of their renewed friendship in her diary.

From a distance, the children watched the Queen as she walked through the halls looking at all of the objects on display until, sometime later, she, along with her elder children, left the exhibition. It would be one of many visits the Queen would make.

After the fanfare of the royal visit died down, the children resumed walking through the great halls. Like the Queen, they too were amazed at what the world's seventeen thousand exhibits of industry and trade had on offer.

As the children walked further along the exhibits, Isabel noticed a long queue of people towards the rear of the building. "I wonder what's going on over there," she whispered to William.

"Let's have a look."

The children made their way over to a very long queue which was abuzz with people chatting enthusiastically. A gentleman tapped William on the shoulder as they walked past. "Young man," he said directly. "You must wait your turn."

"What is going on up there?" asked William.

"Are you not already aware? Why, it's the flushing lavatory. The first of its kind in the entire world."

"You're kidding!" replied William.

"Excuse me?" The man looked perplexed.

"Oh... Er... Why, that is just marvellous," said William.

When the children walked on by, they burst out laughing. "It's a toilet! Everyone wants to see the toilet!"

"Oh no," laughed Isabel, "the *flushing* toilet."

"What a crack up. The things we take for granted, eh, sis?"

When the children stopped to take a breath after laughing so much, a commotion began just behind them. Standing next to an exhibit of guns, a man looked agitated. His American accent bellowed, "Ma Revolver. It's gaaane. Someone has stolen ma revolver!" It was Samuel Colt, inventor of the revolver pistol. On his table he had laid out several new pistols and one had gone missing. As his companions checked under and around the table, people stopped and stared at the flurry of activity. "Where's it gaaane!" he kept repeating over and over again, which caught the attention of the organisers of the exhibition. Soon afterwards, a dozen men, including several policemen, huddled around the exhibit discussing the stolen item.

Stopping to watch the commotion, a loud voice bellowed, "There they are! That's them brats, over there." The children looked around to see where the voice was coming from as two burly men rushed towards them with menacing looks on their faces. Not knowing what to do, they stood there, frozen, hoping the men were talking about somebody else and walk right past them. Instead a big hand landed on William's shoulder and another around Isabel's arm.

"You ain't got not right ta be in 'ere," said one of the men. "Come on then, out you go." He marched the children towards the entrance.

Startled, William said, "We work here, mister. We were carrying the boxes into the entrance over there and, well, my sister wandered off and I was just looking for her."

"Ha! A thief *and* a liar."

"Thief? We're no thieves," snapped William.

"You gotta pay to enter the exhibition," said the man holding Isabel's arm. "Looks like you ain't got no means to pay so off to the work 'ouse you go."

"Workhouse! No! Please no!" yelled William. "Let us go, we live in London. We're locals. Please let us go home."

William and Isabel's protests were ignored and they were marched outside the front door and bundled into a small wagon. William emptied his coat pockets onto the grubby wooden floor. The trophies and other items he took from his bedroom clanked together along with Isabel's yellow watch her mother had given her for her seventh birthday. "Take these," said William, scooping them up and handing them over to the men. "For payment."

"Oh and what 'ave we 'ere then?" said the tall man as he snatched the shiny items from William's hands. "Fink you can pay with this rubbish, eh?" he said as he surveyed the goods. "Hmm, they're worf nuffink, they are," he said and swiftly dropped them in his pocket. "Work'ouse," he shouted towards the front of the wagon. The wagon door slammed shut and the horses trotted away. The magnificent Crystal Palace became smaller and smaller through a little window on the wagon door until it was out of sight.

Isabel began to sob while William hugged her gently. "Don't worry, Izzy, we'll be alright. This workhouse, it can't be that bad – we'll escape, we'll get home."

As the horses clip-clopped through crowded London, they passed market stalls and heard the sounds of everyday life as it was in 1851. Shop workers busied themselves selling everything from fruit and vegetables to carcasses of meat and hog which hung upside down outside shop windows. Men and women wandered up and down the streets, selling their merchandise. The stench of horse manure was overpowering and ladies walked across roads holding up their dresses, dodging the mud and filth that littered the streets. As daylight drew to a close, smoke began billowing out of chimneys. Men dressed in ragged clothes and caps climbed the top of street lamps with small ladders, lighting them with gas. A fog soon enveloped the city and night fell.

The children woke when the horses slowed down. They had been in the wagon all night and slept for most of the long journey. Rubbing their tired eyes, they arrived at the workhouse early in the morning. A big iron gate surrounded the perimeter of the building. The building itself was four storeys tall with rows of windows along the front of the building. A dirt road led horses and wagons to the front of the building. The wagon door opened and a middle-aged woman dressed in a black dress which hung down to her ankles stood there, waiting to receive the children. Her face was pale and her hair was tied up in a bun which sat at the back of her head. It was pulled so tight that looking up at her it appeared as though she had no hair at all. "Mrs Maguire," she said sternly, holding out her hand to little Isabel. "I'll be showin' you round and gettin' you to work." Isabel reached out to the woman as she lifted her out of the wagon. The children were ushered into the building when William told Mrs Maguire there had been a mistake and they weren't supposed to be there. "Ah yes, that's what they all say," Mrs Maguire said nonchalantly. "Come on, then, let's get you started."

The foyer inside the building was rather small in comparison to the building as a whole. Several doors led off into other rooms. The building was divided into two sections, one for men and the other for women and children. There was a small hospital block, separate day rooms and one large laundry. Towards the back of the building were enormous rooms where people worked. The largest rooms were full of machinery where children scooped up cotton from the floor, darting in between heavy weaving machines. It was hot and dusty and the noise from the machines was so loud the children didn't hear Mrs Maguire instructing them to follow her to their dormitory. "Come on, come on," she said as she stood behind them and pushed them along. The children were led up two flights of stairs and through a long corridor which led to their sleeping quarters. Mrs Maguire walked ahead of the children and stopped at a door at the end of the corridor. "This'll be your sleepin' quarters." She motioned as she opened the door. The room was filled with beds, rows of beds, almost touching each other. On each bed was one pillow and a small blanket. Each bed frame had a number on it. Isabel and William stood inside the room. "Right," said Mrs Maguire, "your beds are over in that corner, numbers 242 and 243. Go find them, get changed into the clothes under your bed and make your way back down to the foyer. Mr Babbage will set you to work." As the children slowly made their way to their beds, Mrs McGuire shouted, "Up at 6am, breakfast at 6.15. Dinner at 6pm and bed at 8." And away she went.

Isabel lay on her bed, buried her head in the dank old pillow and began to cry. "I'm sorry, Will," she sobbed.

"Sorry for what?" replied William as he sat next to her and gently hugged her.

"Sorry for getting you into all this mess."

"Don't worry, sis, we'll get out of here. I'm sure we won't be here long. It's not like we have to work off hundreds of pounds of debt, it's just the entry fee at the Crystal Palace. We'll be gone within a week, I'm certain of it."

"I never thought of it like that. Yes, just a week. We *will* be out of here soon."

"If we do what we're told and follow the rules, we should be okay, so let's get changed and return to the foyer."

Isabel wiped her eyes on her sleeves and changed into the old rags from a small box from under the bed. William's clothes were also ragged, his shirt was stained and had holes in it and Isabel's skirt was torn all the way around the bottom. She assumed it had previously been worn by someone much taller than herself, for it hung way below her knees and she wondered what had happened to the previous owner of the dress.

Back in the foyer, the children waited for Mr Babbage and shortly afterwards, the doors from the men's side of the foyer opened and a tall man entered, saw the children and made his way towards them. He wore a black three-piece suit, white shirt and big boots that made a loud clunking noise when he walked across the bare floorboards. Age-wise, he looked about seventy and the hairs at the end of his moustache turned up on either side of his cheeks. A gold chain, fastened to a fob watch on his coat pocket, swayed back and forth as he walked. The closer he got to the children the taller he became and the more sinister he looked. "Good morning," he said. "My name is Mr Babbage and I am the master of this fine establishment. I see you have already met Mrs Maguire, which means you will know the location of your dormitory."

"Good morning," whispered the frightened children.

"I have it on good instruction that you are orphans," he said.

"We are *not* orphans," replied William. "We live with our mother in London. We just went to see the Great Exhibition and a man thought we were stealing, or something, and we ended up here. It's all been a big mistake."

"Please let us go," begged Isabel. "We just want to go home."

"Afraid not," said Mr Babbage. "Your departure is a matter out of my hands. You will work and live here until the age of sixteen at which time you will be free to leave in order to find more suitable lodgings and employment."

"Sixteen!" the children cried.

"In the meantime, during your time here you will be allowed three hours per day to attend school. You will be taught reading, writing, arithmetic and the Christian religion. We have a fine school at this establishment and you should be very lucky to be here instead of walking the streets. Here you will have food and shelter."

"Where exactly are we?" asked William.

"Why, Bristol, of course. Be thankful you were not sent to the Midlands, for those workhouses are older and in need of repair. They are damp and crowded. Why, some of them house eight thousand workers. Here we have two thousand. Now follow me where you'll be put to work."

The children reluctantly followed Mr Babbage. Isabel thought about Mother and how much she wished she was at home. She missed her friends at school, especially Jess, and compared with her current situation, realised home life wasn't that bad after all. William was already thinking of ways to escape the prison that was now their home. Isabel was taken to the kitchens where she was tasked to wash dishes, mop floors and carry out any other duties required of her. There she met Maisie, another child, who, at thirteen, had been working in the kitchens since she was seven. Maisie arrived at the workhouse with her mother who later died of typhoid.

William was put to work sweeping the floors then pulling apart the cotton from the dirt so that it could be reused. He felt lucky enough not to be ducking under the weaving machines as that was a very dangerous job. Some children were too slow getting out from under the machines and became stuck, accidentally killing themselves, while other children lost their fingers. The big room was noisy with the clunk-ker-klunking sound of the machines as the weaving looms moved back and forth. After a few hours, William's bare feet had collected wisps of cotton that got stuck between his toes. The big broom was heavy and its bristles were thick and coarse which gave him sore arms as he swept back and forth.

After spending the remainder of the day carrying out their assigned duties, a bell rang throughout the halls and all of the children from various rooms stopped what they were doing and ran towards the doors. Suddenly, all the doors burst open and the empty foyer was filled with the loud banter of children making their way up the stairs to their dormitories. An exhausted Isabel and William joined them. Their big empty dormitory looked completely different now that it was filled with children. Some lay on their beds, resting, while others sat two or three to a bed, chatting amongst themselves. As soon as Isabel and William walked through the dormitory, the children stopped talking and stared at them. They quietly sat on their beds and waited for dinner.

Next to William's bed, a boy around the same age introduced himself. "Hello. I'm George, George

Frazer." Like William, George also wore ragged clothes. He was a lean figure with curly red hair and freckles across his nose, spanning out over his red cheeks. His hands were chafed with cuts and callouses and his feet were black with dirt.

"I'm William and this is my sister, Isabel."

"Well," said George. "I see you're new here. Stick with me and you'll be fine."

"How long have you been here?" asked Isabel.

"Oh, about three years. I'm an orphan too. Everyone in this room is." Isabel and William looked around at all the children that had no parents. Seeing the looks on their faces, George said, "It's not that bad. We get meals and our own bed. At least here we're not begging in the streets. We get along, most of the time. Where do you come from?"

William told George that he and Isabel were caught at the Great Exhibition. He couldn't tell George who they really were, of course. As George listened intently a second bell rang throughout the halls. "Dinner!" exclaimed George. "Come on, I'm starving." They hopped off their beds and all of the children pushed through the narrow door and ran down the corridor to the dinner room where two long rectangular tables were positioned on either side of the room. The children queued to the front of the room where dinner was being served. A big lady wearing a dirty apron around her enormous waist scooped out stew from a pot whilst another scooped mashed potato. It made a plonking sound as it hit the metal trays. At the end of the queue the children collected their forks, a cup of water and sat down to eat. Isabel looked down at the big gloopy mess that was dinner.

William whispered, "I know it looks awful and it probably tastes awful too but you'd better eat it because we can't afford to get sick."

"I think eating this will actually make me sick," replied Isabel. Slowly she picked up her spoon and began eating. The stew wasn't that bad but the potato mash was lumpy and she had to get it down with big gulps of water. By this time, the hall was full of children sitting, eating and chatting. Mr Babbage entered the room and stood at the front, ensuring the smooth running of the operations. After giving a few instructions to the dinner ladies he swiftly left through a side door.

Later that night, when all the children were fast asleep in their beds, Isabel and William lay wide awake still wondering how on earth they ended up in this mess. They knew they had to escape and soon. For all they knew, the oak tree in the park might lose it's magic one day and then they would be stuck in 1851 forever. Stuck in the workhouse until they were sixteen years old. Then what would they do? Where would they go after that? With no family to go home to, they would be homeless, which would indeed be worse than the workhouse.

"Isabel," whispered William. "Are you awake?"

"I'm awake."

William climbed out of bed and lay down next to Isabel. "We need to hatch a plan to get out of here."

"But how?"

"Not sure yet but we need to get to know this place a bit better. Maybe we can somehow sneak out on a horse and wagon. Surely they must get their supplies from somewhere. You work in the kitchens so your job is to find out how often food gets dropped off. Find out the times and when the wagons leave."

"I think I can do that," whispered Isabel.

"I think that might be our only way out."

"William, please get us out of here."

William pulled his little sister towards him and hugged her. They fell asleep and slept soundly.

Two long weeks dragged on and the children got used to the routine of life in the workhouse. Working in the kitchens, Isabel learnt that large drums of rice and sugar were dropped off every Monday and Thursday. The empty drums were then loaded back onto the wagons, which were sent back to London for reloading. William had found out that all other supplies came from different parts of the country so hiding among the empty drums was their only way home. Over the following weeks, William and George became firm friends while Isabel and Maisie also formed a close friendship. Every morning the girls hid in the kitchen pantry, giggling as they feasted on warm bread as it cooled on racks after being baked in big ovens. The warm bread filled their empty bellies after the tiny rations of porridge they were given at breakfast. If they worked well and managed not to drop food or break anything, Mrs Staunton rewarded them with a small slice of sponge cake and jam that would normally be saved for Mr Babbage. Maisie moved her bed next to Isabel's so they could whisper secrets to each other at night until they fell asleep and in the mornings they tied each other's hair back as was the requirement of all women and girls to avoid any accidents.

One evening, when the children had finished dinner, they walked back to their dormitory, exhausted and dragging their feet. William noticed something shiny fall out of George's shoe as he got changed into his nightshirt. It was a silver coin that fell to the floor and rolled around in circles until it came to a stop when it hit the bedpost. George quickly bent down to pick it up, however it stopped closer to William's bed so he got there first. William scooped up the coin and when he held out his hand to give it back to George, he noticed that one particular side looked very familiar. To his utter shock, it was a picture of Queen Elizabeth II.

CHAPTER 5

William sat on his bed, unable to comprehend just how someone in 1851 was able to acquire a coin with Queen Elizabeth II's face on it when Queen Elizabeth II was not actually born until 1926. It was at this moment he realised that George was also a time traveller. Seeing the total shock on William's face, George guessed that William was now aware that he hid a very big secret and it was time to let him know.

"I guess I have some explaining to do," said George as he sat next to William.

"So do I," replied William. "You see, I was born in the twentieth century and I know you're not from this time either. Isabel and I are here by accident, through a magic tree in Bishops Park in London."

"Oh my gosh!" exclaimed George. "Me too! I saw a glowing tree one day and touched it with my hands and somehow ended up here. A policeman thought I was an orphan and I was sent here."

Isabel was just as shocked as William. "It wasn't the big oak tree that you touched, was it?" she asked.

"I don't think so. It was the big tree next to the pond."

"Right," said William, nodding his head intently. "That would make sense as every tree takes you back to a different year. You see, on one occasion we touched a different tree which took us back to 1945 so we did some research and found out that every magic tree takes you back to the year the tree was planted."

"It's quite unbelievable," George said, his voice quivering. "I just can't believe it."

The children spent the next four hours talking about their experiences with the magic trees in Bishops Park. George told Isabel and William that his grandmother lived on Windermere Road in London and that he was visiting her one afternoon with his mother. Out of boredom, he ventured into the park to have a look around and that's when his time travel began, also ending up in the nineteenth century. George roamed the streets and it wasn't long before a policeman noticed him walking alone and mistook him for an orphan. George couldn't tell the policeman where he came from so made up a story that he was the son of a blacksmith, whom he noticed in a nearby shop window. Unfortunately for George, the policeman happened to know the blacksmith and George was swiftly taken away.

They realised that both George and William were born in the same year, which meant that they could all escape together and that's exactly what the children decided to do. Isabel and William couldn't leave George to spend the rest of his life in the nineteenth century when he belonged in another. So it was decided they would all escape together. William told George about the drums of food coming and going into London and George, having been at the workhouse for three years already, agreed that this would be their best option. The children set their plan in motion for they were anxious to get out of the horrible workhouse and return home to their families. The following Monday, when the wagons arrived before dawn, Isabel, William and George quietly slipped out of their beds and got dressed. Tiptoeing down the hall, everything was quiet as the rest of the children were sleeping soundly. It was still dark outside and the children crept down the stairs into the foyer and towards the kitchen. William popped his head through the doors and noticed several men unloading the drums and rolling them up a ramp into the kitchen.

"We need to hide round the back," William whispered. "The only way outside is through the kitchen." The entrance door to the workhouse was bolted shut with a big padlock hanging from the door handles. They would surely be seen creeping through the kitchen and into the foyer.

"I know another way," said George. "Follow me."

The children backed away from the kitchen doors and followed George to the other side of the foyer.

They crept through an area on the men's side of the workhouse where a door led to a small garden. George lifted the latch ever so quietly and opened the door. Outside they quietly tiptoed along the wall, crouching down in order to be as inconspicuous as possible until they came to the rear of the kitchen. They waited until the men were inside. "Now," whispered George. They got up and ran towards the horses and jumped up onto the wagons, hid behind the drums and sat there in silence. William noticed blood dripping onto the floor of the wagon. Following the trail, he realised it was coming from his hand. He had cut it on one of the drums while trying to squeeze behind it. He tore a section from the bottom of his ragged shirt and wrapped it around the wound. The blood began seeping through the rag so he clenched his fist tightly to stop the blood from seeping through any further.

Shortly afterwards, voices could be heard from the kitchen. "All right, then, see you Thursday, Mrs Staunton," bellowed a loud voice. The kitchen door swiftly shut and the man's shoes crunched on the gravel as walked over to the wagon. He jumped up onto the seat at the front and yelled, "Yar!" A quick jolt and the horses galloped away.

Isabel felt absolutely petrified but the overwhelming feeling of wanting to be back home with her mother kept her from panicking. Windermere Road seemed so far away and she wondered whether she would ever see home again. William wondered how life would be different for him and Isabel after everything they had been through together. He was proving to be a stellar brother to Isabel, looking out for her since their journey began. Looking over at her sitting in the corner of the wagon, he realised how much he loved her. He started to remember her when she was a toddler, holding her hands as she learnt to walk. He remembered how bath time was so much fun as they splashed about with all the bubbles, pretending they were diving for fish and sea creatures. His heart was bursting with love and he felt proud of her for how brave she had been on their journey. William took off his jacket and placed it around Isabel's shoulders. She rested her head on her brother's arm and soon fell asleep. George looked back to the home he had lived in for the past three years and the huge building began fading in the distance as they approached the front gates. He didn't know what to expect from hereon. He still couldn't believe that he met two other children who also travelled through the magic trees. It seemed so unreal and at that very moment, he didn't care one bit. He was grateful to finally leave the hard laborious work that had been such an awful part of his life.

As the boys sat together in the wagon, George chatted to William about how he desperately wanted to get back to school and learn, that he wanted to grow up and have a career but most of all he just wanted to have a normal life again, to continue playing cricket, to see his friends but mostly his parents. He told William if he made it home safely he would never again complain about the dinner his mother served.

After eating porridge slop and stew for the past three years his mother's cooking wasn't that bad after all. He would eat all his vegetables now and thank his mother for providing such a nice meal every night. Thinking about food, George realised he had been stockpiling some food in his pockets the past few days. The children would need something to eat for their journey back home so he began emptying his pockets. He produced a few pieces of bread, fairly stale but edible, three bruised apples and a hessian bag with three sausages. "Well done," said William as he saw the food being laid out on the wagon floor. "Isabel was able to sneak two pork pies so we should have enough to get us to London."

"So..." said George. "What happens when we get back to the trees and into our own time?"

"What do you mean?"

"Well, I mean will we still be friends?"

"Of course we will. We're best friends now, always will be." Pausing for a moment, William asked, "Don't you think it's odd that the three of us all travelled back through the same park?"

"I suppose so," replied George. "Maybe there are other people besides us who have travelled. I guess we just don't know."

An hour later, Isabel woke and the children shared some of the food between them. They saved most of it as they didn't know how long it would take to reach London. William deduced that, as the journey to the workhouse took all night, the journey back to London would take all day, so they sat and waited. The horses stopped every few hours for the coachman to eat and rest. The dirt road was a bumpy one, which made all of the passengers feel a little unwell and the coachman was no exception. When the horses and wagon did stop, the children lay down flat so their heads couldn't be seen. After a weary day, they were finally approaching London where they could hear the rumble of daily life. Hundreds of horses pulled wagons in the streets. The city became busier and louder. The horses and wagon eventually stopped and the coachman hopped down causing the wagon to jerk from side to side. William peered out of the top and saw the coachman walk into an alleyway so he quickly jumped off the back of the wagon and held out his hands for Isabel who jumped into his arms. After setting her down he helped George hop down and they all walked quickly away from the wagon, trying to remain as inconspicuous as possible.

Making their way through the crowded streets, they found a small laneway where they were sure they couldn't be seen by any policemen.

"Where are we?" asked Isabel.

"Somewhere in London but not sure exactly where," replied William, looking around. "Wait! Over there! It's St Paul's. That means we're in central London.

We need to get to the south-west side of the city to get back to Bishops Park."

"We can't walk," said George. "It's too far. We can't risk getting caught either."

"Can you imagine being caught and sent back to the workhouse?" shuddered William. "There's no way other than hitching a lift on a coach."

The children settled down on some crates that had been discarded in the laneway while they thought about how to get across town. It was getting dark and their supply of food was running out. "We only have the bread left," said George as he rummaged through his pockets. They ate the remainder of their food in silence. Realising that trying to get a lift in a stagecoach to the other side of London would be near impossible, the children decided to wait until dark then walk. They crossed their fingers that they wouldn't run into any trouble along the way. William and George decided to take turns getting a bit of sleep before their journey ahead and they thought, as Isabel was so young, she should rest as much as she could.

Before long, it was dark so the three children picked themselves up, brushed off their dirty clothes and stepped out of the laneway. The streets looked quite different from the twenty-first century as they were used to seeing cars and buses driving down cemented roads instead of horses and carriages. They were not used to being in the streets at night either and they all felt frightened. However, they were in luck. After spending the next few hours making their way through the streets of London, on the horizon they could see the top of the dome at the Great Exhibition. "Look, Isabel, we're almost home!" exclaimed William. Passing through Hyde Park, the children looked at the glass structure one last time and soon enough they were at the entrance to Bishops Park.

"Here we are," said George as they all held hands and entered the park together. They were hungry and tired and desperately wanted to return to their homes.

Reaching the oak tree first, Isabel yawned, "This is our tree."

"Mine is over there," said George, pointing over to the pond.

The children said their goodbyes to George. "Don't forget where we live," said William as he hugged his best friend. "Good luck." Into the darkness, George walked towards his tree and was gone.

Isabel and William stood at the base of the oak tree, placed their hands upon its big trunk and closed their eyes. Nothing was happening. The only noise they heard was an owl hooting in the distance. Isabel opened her eyes first. Looking down at her clothes, she still wore the dress, shawl and black boots she was wearing when she entered the nineteenth century. The panic set in and she screamed, "William!" Startled, William opened his eyes. Looking at Isabel, he felt a big lump in his throat that moved all the way down to the pit of his stomach. "What's happening?"

"Oh no!" cried William. "We haven't gone back. It didn't work." Looking around the deathly quiet park, they knew they were still in 1851.

"I just want to go home," cried Isabel as she buried her head in her hands.

"George!" William ran towards George's tree. He was gone. He ran around the tree several times. He scaled the tree, climbing up its branches looking for him. Realising George was well and truly gone, William jumped down from the tree and slowly walked back to the oak tree where Isabel was still standing, waiting for him to return with George. "He's gone, Izzy."

"I don't understand. Why did it work for him and not for us?"

"I just don't know. I don't get it."

Feeling broken-hearted and terrified, the children sat down at the base of the tree. They didn't know what to say, nor did they know what to do. Exhausted from walking through the night, they decided it was best to catch up on some much needed sleep, then they would be in a better frame of mind to decide what to do. Daylight would break in a few hours and they needed to avoid contact with as many people as possible. Sticking together was absolutely essential so they curled up together and fell asleep, cuddling each other in the mild May night. If it had been winter they would have frozen to death. The owl had stopped hooting, which gave rise to a deathly silence within the gates of the park. Regardless of which century they were in, all of London's inhabitants seemed safely tucked up in their beds, in their own homes, in their own time – with their own families.

CHAPTER 6

William woke to the sound of tweeting birds. Sitting up, he looked around the quiet park and wondered what he was doing there. It took a few moments to realise he had woken up in the nightmare of being stuck in 1851. He looked down at Isabel who was still asleep. Not knowing what to do, William looked around the park. The caretaker house looked different, brand new, in fact. Instead of long weeds growing around the porch, the grass was cut short with flowerbeds forming a little stone path leading to a shiny white picket fence. William knew Mr Brown wouldn't be there, for he hadn't even been born and wouldn't for a hundred years or so. He thought it was worth a try knocking on the front door, so he stood up, stretched his legs and walked over to the little house. He quietly lifted the latch on the gate, walked up the little path and stepped onto the porch. The windows on either side of the door looked the same, however, they were clean and lovely. Cream coloured lace curtains hung from inside the windows. He thought the house must have been recently built. After all, the park was fairly new so it made perfect sense that the house would also be new.

William knocked on the door. No answer. He knocked again. Still silence. Peering through the windows, it appeared nobody was home so he turned the door handle and, to his surprise, it opened. "Hello?" William called out. Stepping through the front door, William found himself in the hallway with two rooms on either side. The door to the room on his right was closed. The room to his left had a large round rug covering the floor where a lounge suite and two chairs faced each other with a small wooden coffee table in between. On the table was a silver tray with an empty tea cup, a teapot and small sugar bowl. A small stack of newspapers lay neatly on the floor under the table. William slowly entered the room and looked through the window. For the first time he saw the house from the inside instead of seeing it from the outside. A quaint little desk and chair were perfectly arranged right in front of the window. William nervously walked back into the hallway when he heard a noise from upstairs where a little old lady was standing on the top step. Startled, she took a moment to regard William, lifting a pair of spectacles from a chain around her neck to get a better view. She held out her old and wrinkly hand and clutched the bannister as she walked slowly down the stairs, her stare fixed on William. Her shoes peeped out from under her long black dress, her grey hair neatly tied up in a bun on the top of her head.

Halfway down the stairs, she spoke. "And who might you be?" For a little old lady her voice was quite menacing and William began to feel very uncomfortable. "I said... Who might you be?" she repeated.

"I'm sorry," replied William. "The door was open and..." William stopped talking as he just didn't know what to say. How could he tell the old lady that he and Isabel were stuck in a century they didn't belong in? The old lady was now standing on the bottom step where she was the same height as William. They stood there eye to eye, she, waiting for his answer, and, he, buying some time to come up with a plausible reason to why he would be standing in somebody else's house.

Again, the old lady studied William. "Hmm," she said, peering over the top of her glasses. "Are you lost?"

"Oh yes, lost," William replied. He felt a little relieved that the old lady appeared to sympathise with his predicament.

"I'm Mrs Brown."

"I'm sorry, did you say Brown?" asked William.

"Why, yes, Brown," she replied.

William knew that name, he'd heard it before. Suddenly he remembered Mr Brown was the park caretaker from 2013. It had to be a coincidence, surely he and the old lady weren't related in some way. William wanted to know but was too afraid to ask.

"And who might this young lady be?" the old lady said, looking towards the front door.

William spun around and there stood Isabel at the front door. Her clothes were crumpled and a bright green leaf stuck out of her messy hair. "This is my sister, Isabel," said William as he walked over and held her hand. "It's okay," he whispered to the frightened little girl.

"Well, you had both better come in and have some tea."

The old lady ushered the children into the lounge room where they sat down and waited silently for Mrs Brown to make the tea. She returned with a fresh pot of tea and two extra cups. Sitting opposite the children, she poured the tea and handed a cup to the children. William realised he needed to be careful what he told her. He couldn't talk about computers, cars and especially the oak tree.

"Where are you from?" Mrs Brown asked as she sipped her tea. "I detect you are not from the area."

"Er... We lost our mother at the Great Exhibition," replied William. *Yes*, he thought. *That's a great story. We'll go with that then we won't have to explain ourselves being in a different century.*

Mrs Brown sipped her tea again. The steam fogged up her glasses so she removed them from the tip of her nose, pulled out a handkerchief from her sleeve and began wiping the steam away. "I meant, what *year* are you from?"

William and Isabel were shocked. "Excuse me?" said William.

"What... Year?" Mrs Brown repeated as her voice crackled.

"Just tell the truth, William," said Isabel. "Mother always taught us to tell the truth."

"And where is your mother?"

"If I tell you, you won't believe us," said William.

"I think I just might. You see, I know about the trees in this park. I know they take you to a different place in time."

"Oh, thank goodness for that," sighed William, feeling relieved. "We are from 2013. We found out about the oak tree by mistake. We were trying to get back home but the tree wouldn't take us. It just closed off and now we're stuck here."

The old lady reached over and held William's bandaged hand. "This is why you couldn't return home," she said. "Your hands are the point of entry and they must be in the same condition, whether you are coming or going." William figured it would be at least a week until his hand would heal. "I don't know why it works that way, but it just does," she continued. William sipped his tea while Isabel scooped up a couple of biscuits and ate them hungrily. The old lady poured more tea and the three of them sat in silence, drinking their tea. The children finished the plate of biscuits.

CHAPTER 7

Mrs Brown told the children they could stay at the house in Bishops Park until William's hand was better so they chatted about the park and the trees, all the while not really finding out anything significant, for old Mrs Brown seemed rather vague and was unable to remember much about anything. "An old lady like me doesn't remember much these days," she kept repeating to the children. When Isabel began falling asleep, she thought they might like to rest their sleepy heads so she guided them up the staircase.

The children entered a quaint little bedroom with two small beds separated by a bedside table. The walls were decorated in a soft yellow with white flowers while an oil lamp hung from a hook next to the door. In the corner of the room was a very old looking wardrobe. When Mrs Brown left the children to rest, she shuffled out of the room and gently closed the door. William tried to open the wardrobe but it was locked so he slumped on his bed, looked around the room and opened the draw of the bedside table. Two books sat in the drawer so he picked them up and flicked through the pages. One of the books was *The Holy Bible* and the other was *Jane Eyre* by Charlotte Bronte. Placing the Bible back in the drawer, William had a quick look through the first few pages of *Jane Eyre*. Realising that the book must be a first edition, he knew it would become very valuable in years to come so he gently placed it back in the drawer and closed it. When the drawer shut a key fell from underneath so William picked it up and turned it over a few times wondering why someone would hide a key on the underside of a drawer. There wasn't a keyhole on the bedside table so he assumed it must be the key to open the wardrobe. Isabel, who was resting on her bed, watched William as he walked over to the wardrobe and slipped the key firmly into the lock. It was a perfect fit. He slowly turned the key, trying to make as little noise as possible and all of a sudden the wardrobe opened.

"What's in there?" asked Isabel inquisitively.

"Just a pile of boxes and papers," replied William as he sifted through the contents on the shelves.

Isabel hopped off her bed and joined William as they rummaged through the papers. Most of the contents were old newspapers, lease documents and the odd receipt book. However, a particular document piqued Isabel's attention. "Look, William," she said, holding a small notebook. Written on the front cover was 'Simon Brown'.

"Simon Brown!" said William. "He's the park caretaker in *our* time. How can he possibly be alive in 1851?"

"Well, we still haven't found out how he and the old lady are related," replied Isabel. "Do you think he is a traveller too? I guess that would explain why his name is on this notebook."

"Could be," said William. "I think we should open it."

William opened the notebook while Isabel watched over his shoulder. The first page was a list comprising three columns. In the left column were names of people, the second column had dates, and the third looked like some sort of financial transaction. On the first page the dates began on 25 March 1723. William flipped through the pages and halfway into the book was the last entry which was dated 1898. Some of the names in the book were simply 'Jack' or 'Helena', while other names had surnames.

"I don't get it," said Isabel. "Who do all these names belong to?"

"Beats me."

"Look! The last page! Those are our names!" exclaimed Isabel.

"Oh my gosh," replied William. "And look at the date! It's the 7 May 2013."

"That's the date we travelled to 1851."

William slumped against the bed and sat there, dumbfounded. "She's part of it too," he whispered for fear of being heard by Mrs Brown. "We need to get away from here. And we need to find out who all these people are. They could be in danger."

"Where do we go, Will?"

"I'll think of something. We're taking this book with us," he said as he stuffed the notebook under his shirt.

William quickly placed the boxes and papers back into the cupboard and locked it. He then stood in front of the bedroom door and pressed his ear against it. The whole house seemed eerily silent so the children thought Mrs Brown must have gone out. He and Isabel quietly stepped out of the bedroom and after peering down the staircase for Mrs Brown, who was nowhere to be seen, the children crept down the first few steps, stopping only when a couple of wooden boards underneath them creaked. After regaining their confidence, they crept ever so quietly down each step until they were almost at the front door. Isabel held onto William's arm for dear life. *Just a few more steps*, thought William as he reached his arm towards the door handle.

"You!" bellowed a voice from behind them. The children swung around and in the hallway was none other than Mr Brown. The park caretaker. The children stood in shock for what seemed like ages, although only a few seconds had passed. "You!" shouted Mr Brown again. "What you doin' 'ere?"

William was speechless. Isabel stood, frozen. "I said, what you doin' 'ere?" Mr Brown repeated.

"I... Um... No, what are *you* doing here?" William said. "What's going on here?"

Mr Brown was now standing in the hallway. "You weren't supposed to come back."

"What?" William asked. "You know about the trees?"

"Course I do. How do you think you ended up at the workhouse?"

It was all too much for William. His head was spinning. "How do you know about the workhouse?" he asked.

"You weren't meant to come back!" Mr Brown, now standing with his hands on his hips, looked very angry.

William sensed his fury. "Come on." He grabbed Isabel's hand and ran out the front door. As they ran down the porch steps, Mr Brown kept shouting at them. They couldn't make out what he was saying for he stopped yelling when he realised the children had no intention of coming back. They ran as fast as they could towards the park entrance and ran through the big iron gates. "He knows about us going back! He knows about the workhouse!" exclaimed William. "He was part of it. They both are. She must have been keeping us upstairs so she could get him." Realising they needed to get as far away from the park as possible, the children kept running, flipping mud up with their shoes as they ran as fast as they could through the muddy streets of London.

Back at the cottage, Simon Brown yelled, "They've gone, Ma." He ran back out of the house onto the porch. He scanned the park with his menacing eyes but the children were nowhere to be seen so he returned to the house, sat down on the sofa and threw his hands up into the air. "Gone," he repeated. Mrs Brown, who was standing at the window, holding a curtain open to see what was going on outside, turned around and glared at Simon.

Now with hands on *her* hips, she howled. "And whose fault is that? You weren't supposed to arrive until they were asleep. It was almost done. Now you've ruined it."

"I'm sorry, Ma. I'll find them."

"Yes, you will find them! Yes you will!"

"They can't go too far," said Mr Brown, "they don't have any money."

"They will be sleepy too. Go now and find them."

Unbeknownst to the children, Mrs Brown had mixed valerian leaves with their tea that morning in order to make them very sleepy. She needed them to sleep so that Mr Brown could return them to the workhouse.

Mr Brown was born in 1970 and grew up in the caretaker's house. His father and grandfather were also park caretakers and he was a descendant of Mrs Brown. When Mr Brown was ten, he found out about the magic trees, just as Isabel had. The same phenomenon occurred one day when he saw bright lights around the trees and found that he could travel back in time. A maple tree that had been planted in 1960 became his first journey. After seeing London's vibrant rock and roll scene, Mr Brown wanted to be just like his heroes, The Beatles, and join a band. Life was fun for the young Simon Brown. However, things changed when his mother disappeared when he was fifteen years old. She was never found or seen again so it was assumed she ran away from her husband and young Simon. Simon felt it was his fault that she left and his personality changed soon after. He became introverted and by the time he was thirty, he disliked people altogether. When his father died of old age, he was completely on his own, without friends, without love and without any family. He took over as park caretaker and shut himself away from life. He hated children.

Mrs Brown was born Agatha Blackwell in 1790. Neither she nor Mr Brown knew who the first traveller was or why only some people could travel. It was in 1822 when Mr Brown first met Agatha in the park. She was thirty-two years old. And he was twelve. Agatha had found him wandering around the park. After she realised he was a traveller, she took him under her wing and they became firm friends. She became his surrogate mother when his own mother disappeared.

It was during one of Mr Brown's travels that he, too, ended up in a workhouse in the middle of England. The master of that workhouse was an awful old man named Mr Lewis who worked everyone sixteen hours per day and they were given little else but bread and stale cake to eat. It was an awful time for everyone and it was a common occurrence for people to drop dead from exhaustion right at the spot where they were working. Families were separated from one another and all of the rooms were cold during winter and stinking hot in the summer. Mr Lewis took a particular dislike to Simon Brown, who was made to spend a whole year unravelling strands of old ropes. It was an awful job as the rope was rough and gritty which made Simon's hands bleed. A couple of years later he was taken aside by Mr Lewis and told that the only way he could ever hope to leave the workhouse would be if he kidnapped children and sold them to him. For every child Mr Lewis had under his care, he received a certain sum of money from the owners of the workhouse. This money was supposed to be spent on its upkeep and maintenance, to buy food and water and to clothe and house all of the people living in it. Instead, the money went into Mr Lewis's own pocket. Every night he dined on delicious meals such as rabbit stew, vegetables and potatoes, drank bottles of red wine and lived a life akin to royalty.

He wore a gold fob watch and regularly pulled it out of his pocket to ensure the strict routines of the workhouse were being adhered to. At well over six feet tall, Mr Lewis was menacing. His ears were unusually long with bushy tufts of hair growing out of them. Nobody dared put a foot wrong, which wasn't that difficult as Mr Lewis stomped so hard on the ground he walked on that he could be heard from several rooms away. Everybody knew when he was coming so they had time to work faster and be ready before he entered the room. He spent his days walking from room to room with his cane and would bang it loudly on the floor to get the attention of a worker. He didn't care for names, all he cared about was getting as much work done as possible. 'Work work work' was his motto.

At first, Mr Brown was horrified when Mr Lewis told him he was to procure children for the workhouse. He detested the idea and resisted but soon realised that it was his only way out of the workhouse and to freedom. After a few years, Mr Brown was so used to being under the control of Mr Lewis that he began to think like Mr Lewis. Working directly with Mr Lewis turned him into a very mean person. It also became a good money-earner for Mr Brown. When he became a young man he had the choice to leave the workhouse but Mr Lewis, realising that he would lose most of his ill-gotten income, made a deal with Mr Brown and they agreed to keep the children coming and split the profits equally. Mr Brown, having no family or friends, decided he would continue working with Mr Lewis for the rest of his life. It was perfect. He could travel back to the workhouse to collect his earnings while he lived in the little cottage in Bishops Park, also earning a living as caretaker.

CHAPTER 8

William and Isabel were stuck in 1851 and spent their first night sleeping in an alleyway just around the corner from Bishops Park. They made a makeshift bed with some discarded boxes they found. It wasn't very comfortable but they were glad to be away from the main streets where dangerous people lurked at night. As they huddled together, they listened to the sound of horses trotting and the crackling of fires being lit in the streets by the homeless to keep themselves warm. Most of the alleys and narrow streets were full of homeless people bedding down for the night or wandering around aimlessly with no home to go to. It was lucky that the children found an alley that wasn't as well known as many of the others and they only had to share it with an old man who sat at the other end. He looked too old to be a threat to them and his big hat rested forward on his head, shielding his view of the world.

When Isabel fell asleep, William pulled out Mr Brown's notebook and flicked through the pages. Reading through all of the names, he came across a name that was familiar. It was George Fraser's. Next to his name it was dated 2012, which meant that

George had also been sold to a workhouse by Mr Brown. However, George had been sold to the workhouse that Isabel and William were sent to, which was run by Mr Babbage. This meant that Mr Brown must also be working with Mr Babbage, as well as Mr Lewis, to steal children. William wondered how many other workhouses Mr Brown was working with and how many children he had sold altogether so he decided to do something about it. He was going to help the orphaned children in Mr Babbage's workhouse break free from hard labour and from the awful conditions in which they lived. He knew which children had been sold as all of their names were written in the notebook. He didn't know how he would achieve such a mammoth job of rescuing them but, thinking of his father, about how his father taught him to be the best person he possibly could, he would fight for these children. He would do it for his father. He would make him proud for he always felt that his father was close by, looking down on him wherever he was. William, feeling exhausted, eventually fell asleep as the noise in the nearby streets began to fade away as the homeless, too, went to sleep.

CHAPTER 9

The following day, William discussed with Isabel his plan to free the children and she thought it was a wonderful idea. Realising it was a dangerous mission, they felt scared, nervous, anxious but also happy that they were helping the children who so desperately needed saving. William wondered whether the real reason he ended up in 1851 was to free the orphaned children. Even though he knew he was just another child that had been sold, he had a strange feeling he had been chosen for the mission. Perhaps it was just a coincidence that he injured his hand and couldn't return home, which led him to finding the notebook in Mrs Brown's closet. In any case, his fear began to subside just thinking about all of the children he would help escape. His strength and confidence returned and he now felt that he had a new purpose in life. He thought it was incredible that his way of helping people was through a window of time travel. It was unbelievable, surreal, and he was thankful that he had Isabel to share it with.

William and Isabel knew they had to re-enter the workhouse they had recently escaped from but had no clue how they would return. They could go back to the Great Exhibition and get themselves caught again but there was no guarantee they would end up at the same workhouse. They had to get back the same way they left, on the wagon carrying the big drums. They knew how to get back to the street in London where the wagons refilled their stock, so early one morning they left their alley which had been their home and began the long walk across London. After a long day they finally arrived at the same spot where they jumped off the wagon with George Fraser. Standing in the busy street, William looked around and felt a little sad that George wasn't with them. He missed his best friend but was happy that George made his way home and imagined him sleeping in his own bed again, getting up in the morning and getting ready for school. He wondered whether George thought about him too or whether he had forgotten him already. He hoped they would see each other again one day and had a strange feeling they would.

A tired Isabel sat down on the pavement and leaned up against a railing. Placing her hands on her empty stomach, she realised she hadn't eaten anything all day. William sat down next to her and pulled out an apple and a large cob of bread from the inside of his jacket.

"But how..." said Isabel, surprised.

"Don't ask," replied William and handed her the apple. As the children ate in silence on the sidewalk Isabel noticed the wagon turning into the street. The same driver was perched on the front seat, reigns in hands, guiding the horses into the street as they slowed down. The wagon was full of barrels which meant they had enough time to jump onto the wagon and hide themselves.

"There it is." Isabel pointed to the wagon and they both jumped up and scurried behind the railing, out of view from everyone, including the driver.

He yelled out, "halt!" He pulled the reigns hard and the horses swiftly stopped.

Jumping off the wagon, the driver disappeared into a small store and a few minutes later returned with three more men who helped him pull the barrels from the wagon, tip them onto their side and roll them into the store. As darkness fell, the children waited for the men to emerge and reload the wagon with the empty barrels. When the last barrel had been pulled up onto the wagon, the children made a run for it and quickly hopped up, crawling towards the front and lay there until the wagon made off again.

After a bumpy ride, the children arrived at the workhouse early the following morning. When the wagon pulled up around the back, outside the the kitchen, the children jumped off when nobody was around. They slid into the kitchen where several lanterns lit up the room just enough to see Mrs Staunton entering from a side room. William grabbed Isabel's arm and pulled her under the big table in the middle of the kitchen. They huddled together as they watched Mrs Staunton's feet move around the kitchen. "Come on, Maisie," she hollered. "Help unpack the barrels. Over there, that's a girl."

"Yes, miss," replied Maisie as she entered the kitchen. Shuffling over to the door, Maisie yawned as she waited for the barrels to be rolled up the wooden ramp and into the kitchen. When the men removed the big wooden lids, Maisie began pulling out bags of flour, rice and other condiments, and carried them over to the storeroom. Mrs Staunton and the driver disappeared into Mrs Staunton's office where the driver removed his cap, pulled out a logbook from his pocket and handed it to Mrs Staunton, who placed a pair of small glasses on her nose, produced a quill and signed the bottom of the page.

"Quick, let's go" whispered William. Popping his head out from under the table, he looked both ways and crawled out with Isabel right behind him.

Maisie heard the whispers, turned around and saw Isabel crawling on the floor towards the door. "Oh my!" she said in total shock, dropping a bag of flour onto the floor. William turned around and put his finger over his mouth at Maisie. She knew what that meant and returned the gesture with a nod. With flour spilt over the floor Maisie bent down to clean up the mess. Scraping the flour into a little pile, she whispered, "What happened to you?"

Isabel wrapped her arms around her and hugged her tightly. "I can't say right now," she replied. "We'll explain everything later. We need to get back to the dorm."

"You'd better hurry. Everyone will be up soon."

William and Isabel crawled out of the kitchen and headed for their old dormitory upstairs, creeping along the edge of the big staircase until they reached their room. Opening the door slowly, they scurried into their beds and waited until the bell rang. They joined the children in the breakfast hall, collected a tray each and stood in the queue, waiting for the big wooden spoon of slop that was called porridge. William looked around and everything appeared normal. They had been gone only a few days so hopefully their departure hadn't been noticed by Mr Babbage.

As the children sat down and began to eat hungrily, a large figure appeared behind them. It was Mr Babbage. His shadow covered half of the table where the children sat and his loud thunderous voice rang out. "You two! Come with me." The room fell silent and all of the eyes in the room locked on William and Isabel. Mr Babbage grabbed their arms, pulled them out of their seats and marched them out of the room through the hallway and into his office. "Sit," he said, pointing to two big chairs in front of his desk. The children did what they were told. Mr Babbage walked around the opposite side of the table, stood in front of his chair and pulled out a drawer from his desk. Rummaging around the drawer, he produced a pipe and a box of matches.

Lighting the pipe, he puffed, drew a deep breath and blew smoke towards the children.

"Well now," he said as he sat on his big red leather armchair. "It appears we have two runaways. I don't take too kindly to my workers who think they can do whatever they wish. More so," he went on, "workers who are *children* who think they can do whatever they wish. Do you think you can come and go whenever you please?"

"We're sorry, s-sir," stammered William. "It won't happen again, sir."

"And where might George Frazer be?"

The question startled William. He couldn't think of a response quickly enough.

"I am aware he ran away with the two of you. Where did he go?"

Isabel and William glanced at each other wondering what to say.

"Answer me!" yelled Mr Babbage as he slammed his hand down on the big mahogany desk. It made the children jump out of their seats.

"He... Er..."

"He drowned!" cried Isabel. "He fell into the Thames and we couldn't help him out so he drowned."

Good one, Isabel, William thought, hoping Mr Babbage would believe her.

"I see." Mr Babbage walked over to the window, puffing on his cigar, and peered outside where a dozen men were tending to a large field of fruit and vegetables. He stood there in silence for a few moments, just staring. The only noise was the ticking of a clock on the desk.

"Well then," he said. "Owing to Master Fraser's demise in the Thames, one less worker means you two will have to do his new job I was about to assign before he ran away." From the sarcasm in Mr Babbage's voice, it was evident that he didn't believe their story. "Do you know what Master Fraser's new job is?" he asked.

"No, sir." William had a feeling that George's job was going to be worse than the ones they had.

"A scavenger. Do you know what a scavenger does?"

"No, sir" replied William.

"Well then. Let me enlighten you." It was clear Mr Babbage was enjoying every minute of the fear he instilled in Isabel and William. The more he spoke, the more nervous and frightened they felt. "A scavenger spends their day collecting all the loose cotton from under the textile machines. They spend all day on their knees crawling around and sometimes they're not quick enough and end up being crushed by the machines." The children gasped in horror. "Such is life," said Mr Babbage, smiling. "You will do this every morning after breakfast until lunchtime then you will carry out your regular duties from thereon until dinner. Now go and report to Mrs Maguire immediately."

Isabel and William quickly stood up and walked out of the office. They couldn't wait to get as far away from Mr Babbage as possible. Holding hands, together they walked through the corridor and back to the breakfast room where the rest of the children were lining up to return their dirty bowls and spoons for washing. Breakfast was finished and William and Isabel had hardly eaten anything. Mrs Maguire rounded up the children and instructed them to go directly to their workstations. She had already been briefed by Mr Babbage as she pulled Isabel and William aside and marched them over to the rooms that housed the cotton machines. A couple of small barefoot children darted in and out from under the machines, scooping up the cotton as it fell on the floor. The room was hot and dusty and the machines were noisy. There was no ventilation except for a few open windows which didn't seem to make much difference at all.

"There," said Mrs Maguire, pointing to a machine at the back of the room. "Jack at machine number three will show you what to do." She left the room and the children slowly walked over to a young boy who looked no more than ten years old. Fear and panic were the only words that could describe what William and Isabel were feeling.

"Come on," said Jack, "it's not that hard, you just have to get back before the machines." All three children scrambled under and began scooping up the cotton. It was without a doubt the most awful day of their lives.

CHAPTER 10

William had no time to think about how he would rescue all of the orphans from the workhouse. At dinner that evening he looked around at all of the children and wondered which ones had been sold by Mr Brown. After carrying out a quick headcount, he counted twelve children. He wondered how he would return them all to their families, if in fact, they had any. It was a mammoth task, an impossibility, yet he couldn't leave any of the children to a life of hard labour. And what of the children who were born in the 1800s and were not there because of Mr Brown? The children who actually didn't have parents and lived in the workhouse because they were homeless? If he rescued those children they would be still be homeless. That night, when all the children were sleeping, he crept around the room and wrote down their surnames as they appeared on a chalkboard at the end of every bed. He then cross-checked those names and compared them with those in the notebook. Nine of those names matched the names in the notebook, which meant that only three children were actually born in the 1800s – Tommy Nicholson, Albert Parkes and Maisie Donaldson, the kitchen hand who befriended Isabel. Well, William thought, the advantage of knowing who these children were meant that he could help rescue them too. If they had no family perhaps William and Isabel could help them in some way. William felt exhausted and placed the notebook under his mattress. Looking at his injured hand, he could see that it was healing nicely. The wound had closed and he felt sure it would be completely healed within a couple of days. Then he would be able to travel back through the oak tree. He, Isabel and ten more children.

William lay down on his bed and soon fell into a deep sleep. A few hours later, he woke to a loud banging noise coming from downstairs. He sat up and noticed some of the other children had also woken and were sitting upright in their beds looking around at each other, waiting for someone to say something. "What was that?" asked Tommy. William, being the eldest in Dormitory A, felt it was his duty to investigate. He hopped out of bed and crept towards the door, opened it a few centimetres and peered out, looking left, then right. Nothing out of the ordinary so far.

Some of the children also hopped off their beds and started to make their way towards the door. "Back to bed," whispered William. "I'll go downstairs and find out what's going on."

As the children scurried back to their beds William made his way through the dark hallway and down the stairs. He stopped at the foot of the stairs when he saw a shadow standing at the main entrance door, at the other side of the foyer. It was difficult to see what was happening in the dark, however, on closer inspection, the shadow appeared to be a man. Although William could only see the back of him, it was clear he was a worker as his clothes were torn and dirty. In his left hand he held a blunt instrument which he was using to pick the lock that was tightly bolted around a huge metal chain hanging from the door. William couldn't see his right hand, yet it appeared the man was trying to escape. The loud bang must have been the man dropping the instrument onto the floor. As everyone slept, the sound of the instrument would have likely been heard throughout the halls. William heard footsteps coming. He knew the punishment for being out of bed was food rations so he turned around and quickly ran back up the stairs. Reaching the top of the stairs, he heard scuffling noises and the man from downstairs cried out. He couldn't hear what was being said but the man was yelling and screaming. He was promptly dragged away, a door slammed, then silence.

When William returned to his dormitory the children were all sitting on their beds waiting for his news. "Someone was trying to escape," William told the children.

Jimmy piped up with, "Was it the man with one hand?" William looked at him a little perplexed when it dawned on him that the man did indeed have one hand, which was why he couldn't see his right hand. "You see," Jimmy continued, "he's done it before."

"Escaped?" asked William.

"Oh yes. He lost his hand when he first arrived and he's been trying to escape ever since."

"He's a nice man," said Alice from the other side of the room. "Sometimes he plays with us in the garden and one day snuck us some ginger biscuits."

"I'd like to meet him," said William. "If he knows this place well, then perhaps he can help us escape."

"Escape?" the children gasped. They all looked around at each other and their tired little eyes were now brimming with excitement. Soon enough, the children were all huddled around William's bed waiting in anticipation to hear him say the word 'escape' one more time.

William and Isabel explained their story about their travel through the oak tree to the children.

"Me too," said Jimmy.

"Same here," interrupted another. Soon all of the children were yapping on about their own time travel experiences and how it had all began in Bishops Park. They hadn't mentioned it to William or Isabel until now as they were not sure how or why William and Isabel ended up at the workhouse.

When the children were informed of two new children arriving, they decided not to say anything in case the newcomers told Mr Babbage, then they would all be punished for making up silly stories. Their secret was still safe and all they had to do now was escape.

Realising it was well after midnight, the children made a pact never to tell anyone else of their plans to escape or how they ended up in the workhouse. As the three children who were born in the 1840s had no parents or family so it was decided that they would go with the rest of the children through the trees. William promised he would help find them a home where they would be loved, where they would have the opportunity of attending school and building a life for themselves. So it was decided that each and every child in Dormitory A would have a little extra work to do during their day. They would all have to work together to find a way to escape by any means possible. They couldn't escape through the kitchen and onto the wagons again as the barrels were big and took up most of the space. A few children could squeeze between them but certainly not all of them at the same time.

Fourteen-year-old Roger Smith worked in the infirmary changing the bed linen and mopping floors and he knew where the medicines were kept. His idea was to poison Mr Babbage at night or slip something in his brandy to make him sleep. It was a great idea, according to William, who was now the leader of the group. However, even if they escaped they would have no transport into London and walking was out of the question as it was a hundred-mile journey. It would take weeks to walk that far, and would prove impossible for the smaller children. They had to find a way out using a means of transport.

Out of all the children, it was Matthew Evans who had the job of folding the big sheets of cotton cloth and stacking them into large baskets ready for dyeing. Fortunately for the children, this particular cotton mill did not produce the dyes for the material so they had to be sent to another factory for this process to take place. As it happened, the dying took place in London. Matthew relayed every part of his job to William, from his arrival in the morning into the room where all of the finished materials lay sitting in a big pile, to laying them out on the floor, folding them into small squares and placing them in big baskets. He then wheeled them out a back door, down a ramp and left them for collection every Monday, Wednesday and Friday, onward bound for London. It was brilliant, William thought. And it was the only way.

CHAPTER 11

Twelve children, William kept thinking as he worked, weaving in and out from under the machines, collecting shards of cotton. Thinking positively made his days bearable. The mere prospect of escaping the workhouse for good and never having to go back put a smile on his face and he felt encouraged that he could help all of the children in his dormitory. After their secret was out, they had all become firm friends, just like a little family. The older children looked out for the younger ones and William looked out for everyone. Knowing how dangerous the scavenger job he and Isabel were assigned was, he only let Isabel collect cotton from the front of the machines as there was much less chance of getting hurt. He was glad that he had grown to be almost six feet already as it made his job manageable, however exhausting it was.

After two weeks of careful planning, the children of Dormitory A felt ready to make their move. Every evening when dinner was over, they had an hour of recreational time and figured this hour was the best time to escape as they had less chance of being noticed by any of the staff. Mr Babbage usually ate his dinner in his private rooms and wouldn't see the workers again until the following morning.

Matthew Evans had spent his day folding up the sheets of cotton but only filling up half of the baskets. He needed to create space for the children to hide as well as lightening the load so not to arouse suspicion from the men loading the baskets onto the wagons. They had to be exactly the same weight as usual so two children was the maximum they could hide in each basket. Maisie had secretly been storing extra food in her pockets from the kitchen. She was able to hide bread rolls and some fruit in her clothing for the journey back to London. She cleverly sewed little pockets on the insides of the girls' dresses in order to store extra food.

At seven o'clock one evening, William sat at the top of the stairs and waited nervously for one of the workers to take Mr Babbage his dinner. He knew the usual routine and after a few minutes of waiting in silence a young woman appeared carrying a tray. Walking through the foyer, she balanced a bottle of wine and a glass, which clattered together as she walked slowly towards Mr Babbage's room. When she reappeared, empty handed, William knew this was their cue to get moving so he ran back to the dormitory where all eleven children were waiting for him. They were dressed in every item of clothing they possessed in order to keep warm from the chilly evening air. Their pockets were filled with the food Maisie had been storing for them. They brushed their hair, the boys wore their caps while the girls did their hair in plaits and ponytails so that they would look like they belonged to a family, perhaps a poor family but at least they tried their best to belong to somebody to avoid being caught again.

"Well done, everyone," said William as he looked around at all the children. "Now, remember what I told you. Walk very quietly down the stairs and ensure that when you hide in the baskets you keep very still until the horses leave the workhouse. I'll be the first one out at the other end and I'll give you the signal when to hop out." The children all nodded their petrified little heads but looked up to William and put every bit of faith in him. "Let's go." William scooped up his belongings from his bed and stuffed them into his coat pockets.

Tiptoeing quietly out of the dormitory, the children left their room for the last time. None of them took a look back at the empty, desolate room. They were glad to leave a place where nobody loved them, where they only had each other. This was it. They were all going, it was finally happening. William's hand had healed nicely, the bandage was off and he felt confident that very soon he would be back in Bishops Park wrapping his arms around the big oak tree, hearing the bristling leaves and feeling the ground shaking as it took him and Isabel home.

The children crept single file down the big staircase. The younger children walked behind William and the older children last. The foyer was silent. The adults were housed in smaller buildings at the back of the workhouse so it was usual for the foyer to be relatively empty in the evenings, except for a few kitchen staff and anybody who was assigned the slavish task of waiting hand and foot on Mr Babbage. At the bottom of the stairs, William looked around to see if anybody was coming. Mr Babbage was still in his room so they all scurried across the foyer to the other side and straight out the back door to where the baskets were waiting to be carried onto wagons. The baskets were almost empty, except for a few layers of cloth in which to hide the children. William and Matthew helped the children climb into the baskets and covered them up. When they were all tucked away and hidden out of sight, William and Matthew climbed into the two remaining baskets and lay still. So far so good. Everything was falling into place. The plan was working perfectly.

A little while later, most of the children had fallen asleep and didn't notice that they were being hoisted up onto several wagons. Again, William heard the voices of several men. The horses were ready to go and when all of the baskets were in place, the sides of the wagons were bolted up to ensure the goods remained in place.

After a brief silence, a voice started screaming from inside the foyer. "The children are gone! The children are gone!" It was Mrs Maguire screaming through the hallway.

Mr Babbage ran out of his room, a napkin still hanging from his collar. "What is the matter?" he roared.

Mrs Maguire was in a panic, her arms up in the air, she yelled again, "They're gone!"

"Calm down, woman. Who is gone?" he bellowed.

"The children from Dormitory A. I've searched everywhere."

William's heart began thumping when he heard the commotion going on inside. Instinct told him to keep calm but the younger children, hearing that Mr Babbage was now aware that they were missing, might panic or, worse, start crying. *Oh, please*, William thought. *Please get us out of here.*

The riders climbed up onto their seats and the horses were off. As the horses galloped away, the screaming voices of Mrs Maguire and Mr Babbage slowly faded. Soon the only noise was the sound of the horses' hooves and the baskets as they rattled on the floor of the wagons. William knew they were not out of danger yet, as Mr Babbage would have everyone at the workhouse looking for them and when they realised they were gone it wouldn't take much to work out how they had escaped.

The horses slowed down as they approached Bristol train station, a large brick building with tracks running on either side heading north and south. A big steam train was waiting at the platform while a number of men loaded their goods onto the train, pushing heavy boxes up ramps and onto the carriages. Men, women and children also waited to board the train. The platform was abuzz with people coming and going. William peeped out of his basket to see what was going on. He didn't realise their journey to London would be on a train but this was a bonus as they would arrive in London much sooner than expected. He slid back under the cloth when he heard the unlocking of the sides of the wagon. As each basket hit the ground with a thump, the sleeping children woke but remained quiet. They were wheeled up a ramp into a carriage where each basket was placed at the end of the carriage. The big door on the side of the train slammed shut.

CHAPTER 12

Slowly the children began climbing out of the trolleys. William instructed the children to pull all of the cloth from the trolleys and they began making beds with them, keeping to the back of the carriage just in case the train was scheduled to make another stop before arriving in London. They couldn't afford to be seen by anyone, especially now that it would be widely known they were the children who had escaped from the workhouse. By now, every adult in Bristol would be on the lookout. William didn't know how long it would take the train to reach London, nor did Matthew. All Matthew knew was that the cloth went to London for dyeing. William thought the train must arrive at Kings Cross, if in fact Kings Cross station actually existed in 1851. The children had never been on a steam train before. Sitting in their little cloth beds all huddled up together, William told them a story about a very important man named Isambard Kingdom Brunel, a pioneering railway engineer, who designed this railway.

"Oh I've heard of him," said Maisie. "I saw Mrs Staunton reading about him. She told me he was very important because now people could travel all over the country."

"Can't you read?" asked Isabel.

Maisie hung her head in shame and looked at the floor. "No," she replied.

"It's okay," said Isabel, putting her arm around her. "I'll teach you."

"Really? You would?"

"Of course, it's not that hard. When we get home you can even go to school."

"Oh that would be grand," replied Maisie excitedly.

The children spent much of the evening chatting and eating the food they snuck from the workhouse. It was enough to last them a couple of days. By the time they ran out, they should be back in their own homes eating meals with their own families. They shared stories about their families, their school friends and compared life as it was in the twenty-first century to life in the nineteenth century. One by one, the children fell asleep, their bellies full of food and their hearts full of hope. The train chugged its way to London, stopping at Bath and Reading to load more goods.

The children were fast asleep when the train arrived at Paddington station. Maisie woke first and nudged Isabel who sat up, rubbed her eyes and shook William's arm. "William, we're here," she whispered. William opened his eyes and saw the carriage in the light of day. All the crates that were already in the carriage when they arrived remained in the exact spot when they left Bristol so he was quite sure that nobody had been in the carriage and seen them.

"Right then," he said, "let's pack up our stuff and get out of here." All of the children followed William's instructions and folded up the cloth they used as beds and placed them back into the baskets.

Knowing it would be easier to escape from a station that would be packed with people than it would a warehouse where possibly everyone knew who was coming and going, the plan was for the children to make their way back to Bishops Park from the station. Together William and Matthew grabbed the handle on the big door and pushed with all their strength. It moved a few inches but it proved too heavy to open on their own so all the children rallied behind them and all pushed together. The door opened a few more inches and a few more until the gap was big enough for them to stand side on and step out. Looking towards the front of the train, all of the passengers had already disembarked so the platform was relatively empty. A stationmaster was standing at the front of the train, talking to the driver. He held a logbook and was too busy scribbling down notes to see the children. One by one, they stepped onto the platform and walked to the rear of the train. When they reached the tracks, they jumped over them, dodging trains departing from platforms and ran off into the distance.

CHAPTER 13

In Bristol, the workhouse was a flurry of activity. More so than usual as there were twelve people missing. Mrs Maguire was aghast that the children under her care managed to evade her. Mr Babbage was livid. Twelve less people, regardless of age, meant that production would slow down. There were two less bodies to scurry under the machinery collecting cotton. There weren't enough hands in the kitchen to mop the floors, scrub the pots and unpack the deliveries. *No*, Mr Babbage thought, *it just won't do. The children must be punished.* Pacing up and down the foyer and throughout the halls, he rambled on and on to himself and occasionally punched the air with his fist. He shouted at anybody who got in his way and when his lunch was served, he threw the whole tray against the wall. Glass shattered, liquid spilt, food slopped down the wall and landed in a mushy pile on the floor. Nobody dared go near him; nobody had seen him this mad before. Everybody went about their jobs with extra care as they were too scared to make mistakes of their own, for the consequences would be far greater than usual.

"We will no doubt haves to inform the owners," said Mrs Maguire as she sat down with Mr Babbage to discuss their predicament.

"We'll do no such thing," he retorted. "That would mean less funding."

"But, sir, it would be illegal not to report it. We would be breaking the law."

"Oh poop to the law! I am the law!" he shouted.

Mrs Maguire sat in her chair, utterly stunned. Listening to Mr Babbage carrying on about being above the law and how ready he was to break it for the sake of a few pounds that went into his own pocket, she suddenly realised she could not stand the man any longer. After sixteen years of being shouted at, picked on and ordered about, she could no longer take any more. Mrs Maguire stood up and brushed the creases from the front of her dress. Standing right in front of the tall empowering figure in front of her, she no longer felt afraid of him.

"What are you doing?" he said. "Sit down."

"Sir," she said in a soft voice, "I will not sit down. I will not be yelled at. I will not be treated like a peasant any longer. I hereby resign."

"What! What! Resign? You've gone mad, woman! Nobody resigns in *my* employment!"

"Good day, sir."

As Mrs Maguire walked over to the door of Mr Babbage's office, he began yelling, "Come back now! I will not allow this!"

Stopping at the door, she turned around and stared at Mr Babbage. He stopped yelling. "I can only assume they are on their way to London," she said, "and I will find those children and help them. I will help them in any way I can." She left the room and slammed the door shut behind her.

Mr Babbage sunk down in his chair. It was all falling apart. The youngest workers under his supervision had escaped, which made him look ridiculous and his trustworthy assistant had also left. His level of authority was now under question and he wondered how his workers would perceive him. He had spent years perfecting himself into a ferocious persona and now everyone would be laughing at him.

Mrs Maguire stepped into the foyer and breathed a huge sigh of relief. It was as though a very dark cloud had lifted from her shoulders. She felt a certain happiness that had been missing for many years. Her husband died of cholera eighteen years ago and in the following months, she struggled financially. After accumulating debts in order to survive on her own, the only way she could pay back the debt was either end up in debtors' prison or work for Mr Babbage. It was Mr Babbage who paid off her debts as he was her uncle and she was indebted to him since that very day the police arrived at her doorstop to take her to prison. It took ten years to pay back Mr Babbage. The meagre wage she earned went directly to him then when her debt was cleared, she saved every penny she earned for the next six years until she saved enough to leave the workhouse and rent a small cottage. However, she stayed at the workhouse for so many years because she felt she owed Mr Babbage because he saved her from prison. Many people didn't make it out of prison because the conditions were so severe. Disease was rife and if one did survive typhoid or cholera, they would not be segregated from the most awful people of society: muggers, murderers and the insane. Nobody was safe. At least now she could finally break free and live a happy life. Realising just how nasty Mr Babbage was, she wanted more than anything to make amends for the way he treated the children. She had to find them and quickly. Hurriedly, she walked down the big corridors to the small room where she slept. Her room was dark and damp. A small fireplace in the corner kept her warm in winter, yet Mr Babbage didn't allow her to light a fire between the months of April and October as it cost too much money to burn wood and kindling. Opening a small wardrobe next to the bed, Mrs Maguire pulled out a bag and proceeded to pack everything she owned, which wasn't much. She had two identical black dresses that she wore around the workhouse and slept in a nightgown. A few sketches of her late husband sat on a dresser and she placed them in a bag after wrapping them up carefully in an old newspaper. After she packed up sixteen years of her life, she stood at the threshold and looked around the room. She then walked out and shut the door behind her.

Walking to the front entrance, she heard a familiar voice. "Please, can you help me?" Turning around, she saw the man who had previously tried to escape. It was the man with one hand. He stood there, dishevelled, wearing grey trousers and an old shirt, both ripped and dirty. He held out his hand and spoke in a soft voice, "Please help me. I don't belong here."

"None of us belong here," Mrs Maguire replied. "I don't know what I can do for you."

"Take me with you," he begged. "Please. Wherever you are going, I can go with you and offer my protection."

"What do you mean?" she asked.

Looking down at the small bag, the man deduced that Mrs Maguire was going on a trip. "A woman travelling alone is a dangerous business. Take me with you and I will protect you."

Mrs Maguire hadn't thought of the dangers she might face while making her way to London. The walk to Bristol train station would take at least an hour and walking there on her own would prove dangerous. Highway robbers were common and people were occasionally killed for their possessions.

"All right," she agreed. "I'm going to London. You can walk me to the train station and then you must find your own way."

"Oh, thank you and bless you," the man replied.

She pulled out a large silver key and opened the big wooden door just enough for the two of them to slip through. They hurried down the muddy path where the horses and carts trotted to and fro and through the big entrances gates and onto the main road.

"I'm David."

"Catherine Maguire."

"Mrs Maguire, it's nice to make your acquaintance."

"What happened to your hand?"

"I lost it three years ago." Looking at his stump, he continued, "I can't feel anything now, of course."

"You poor man." Mrs Maguire felt sorry for him. A man without a hand would have a difficult life if he was expected to work and support a family.

"Do you have family?" she asked.

"I did once. They are gone now."

Looking at David, Mrs Maguire noticed a tear run down his cheek. She could tell he was a broken man. "Where will you go once we reach the station?"

"I would also like to go to London to find my family but I don't have any money."

They walked the remainder of the journey in silence. Several horses galloped past pulling big black coaches, the occupants looking straight ahead. A little girl wearing a yellow bonnet stuck her head out of a coach window to get a better look at the couple when her mother quickly pulled her back in.

A big clock at the train station began ringing. It was three o'clock in the afternoon. Inside the station, the roof was high with big arches above two platforms. A train was waiting at the departures platform and steam billowed out of a big iron funnel at the front of the train. Mrs Maguire and David made their way to the ticket stand where an older gentleman dressed in a black suit and black cap sat behind a window dispensing tickets.

"Well, I guess this is goodbye," said David as he held his hand out.

Mrs Maguire looked down at his hand, turned to the ticket master and said, "Two tickets for London please."

"Oh, Mrs Maguire," gasped David. "You don't have to do this."

"Do you want to find your family or not?"

"Oh yes I do, so desperately. I don't know how to thank you."

"Just find them. That will be enough."

"Five shillings each for first class or four shillings for third, miss," said the ticket master.

"Two for third please." Mrs Maguire pulled out a small coin purse and counted the coins.

"Off to see the Great Exhibition then?"

"Something like that," she replied as she collected the tickets.

The couple walked to the end of the platform where a sign read 'third class'. Mrs Maguire remembered someone in the workhouse talking about a new train line that had recently been built. The public called it the 'GWR – God's Wonderful Railway', which actually stood for 'Great Western Railway'. Settling into their seats, David turned to Mrs Maguire. "I am so deeply grateful for your kindness and generosity. It's been a very long time since someone has showed me kindness."

"I assume you are referring to the workhouse."

"Yes. Awful place."

"Mr Babbage is my uncle and today is the day I realised he is my uncle only in name, and nothing more."

"Where are you going then, if you don't mind me asking?"

"I am going to find some children who ran away from the workhouse," she said and burst out crying. "I have absolutely no idea how I'll find them but I owe it to them."

"Aah yes, I heard some children had ran away. Well I hope you find them," said David. He soon fell asleep and several hours later, they arrived at Paddington station.

CHAPTER 14

It was eight o'clock in the evening and the sun was setting. It had been a warm and sunny day in London, unusually warm for the month of May. The streets of Paddington were slowing down after a busy day of street trading. Ladies stacked their flowers into baskets and men packed up their boxes of fruit and vegetables. They would all soon be gone and the street would be quiet until early the next morning when the street vendors would return for another day.

Mrs Maguire and David were tired and walked the streets in search of lodgings where they could stay the night and eat a nice warm dinner. They found an inn which looked like a small house with a thatched roof. A sign was nailed to the front door that said 'Travellers welcome'. Inside the hallway, an old lady greeted her guests. She assumed from the way David was dressed that they were not a married couple so she offered Mrs Maguire a room for the night, however, there were no other rooms available. The Great Exhibition was so busy that, since its opening, people from all over the country ventured down to London and, in turn, most of the inns and hotels were fully booked. The old lady told David she was a Christian and never turned away someone in need of a bed for the night so she let him sleep on a cot bed in the corner of the kitchen. After eating pork pies and apple crumble for dinner, Mrs Maguire retreated to her room while David was shown the direction of the kitchen. Most of the diners had finished their meals so the kitchen closed for the night, with the exception of a teenage boy who was finishing up washing the remainder of some pots and pans. All of the cooking had warmed up the kitchen and David climbed into bed feeling full and content for the first time in three years. He was so glad to finally be free from the workhouse that any situation would be better than working sixteen-hour days and sleeping in a cold and damp room. Not knowing what the future held for either David or Mrs Maguire, they decided that they would go and see the Great Exhibition the following morning to cheer themselves up. Mrs Maguire booked a further week's lodgings at the inn, which gave her a place to stay while she looked for the children. Trying to find one or two children in a big city would prove very difficult, yet finding twelve children all travelling together would be easier as they would have more chance of standing out.

The two adults ate breakfast together. Porridge with warm milk was served by a young girl of no more than seventeen or so. Her short brown hair sat just below her ears and she wore a grey dress with a white apron. She introduced herself as Bessie and told Mrs Maguire it was her mother who owned the inn. She poured tea from a big pot and both David and Mrs Maguire thought it was the loveliest cup of tea they had ever drank. A hackney carriage picked them up from the street and took them all the way to Hyde Park. After paying the fare and waiting in line for a very long time, the two finally entered the big glass doors of the Great Exhibition. They walked around for hours, amazed at all the sights. Looking up onto the first floor, they saw Queen Victoria sitting at a table with Prince Albert, tucking in to tea and scones. It was a such surreal experience, being so close to royalty, that Mrs Maguire just stood and stared at the Queen for five whole minutes. The only adult in her life had been her wicked uncle, Mr Babbage, and yet here she was standing in front of the Queen of England. *What a wonderful woman,* she thought as she moved on and rejoined the crowd.

As the two moved around the stalls, they realised they were nearing the end of the exhibition. It was time to move on and as they slowly made their way towards the exit, something caught David's eye. A short man was standing a few feet away, chatting to a group of men. He was playing with a small shiny object that glimmered as he spun the chain around his index finger. The man, joking with his male companions, began laughing and lost his grip of the object. It fell onto the floor and rolled away until it eventually stopped near David's foot. David looked down and realised the object was a fob watch. He bent down and picked up the shiny object and turned it over. The inscription read 'W.P. My greatest love'. He read it over and over again. He couldn't believe what he was reading. It was the fob watch that belonged to his father, Wilbur Pritchard. David had passed it onto his own son, William. Shaking uncontrollably, David knew that William had been to the Great Exhibition. It was at this moment that he realised his own son was a traveller.

"Oh no," he muttered to himself. "It can't be... It isn't possible."

Mrs Maguire saw the colour drain from David's face and quickly ushered him out of the building, leaving the short man scurrying around on all fours, looking for his lost treasure. Outside, Mrs Maguire asked, "Are you all right?"

"This watch," David replied. "It belongs to my son!"

"Your son? How is that possible? Why, you just found it on the floor."

"Yes I know," replied David. "They were here! I just can't believe it." He sat down and leaned up against the glass building. Looking up towards the sky he felt sick to his stomach wondering what on earth William was doing in 1851. His thoughts quickly turned to Isabel. "Oh Isabel," he cried, tears streaming down his cheeks. He prayed to God that his children were safe. Knowing that William knew how to travel through the trees, he hoped they had returned to their mother but in his heart he felt that William was in trouble.

Mrs Maguire held out her hand. "Come. We must find your son."

David clasped her hand tight and picked himself up. "I also have a daughter who might be with him."

"Well then. We must return to the inn where we can make some enquiries. As we are both looking for lost children, it will be a joint venture."

CHAPTER 15

Mrs Maguire and David returned to the inn late that afternoon. Bessie was busy clearing tables after the lunchtime crowd. Realising that Bessie would be around the same age as William, Mrs Maguire wondered if Bessie might know where a teenager would spend their time. After all, she would know the Paddington area relatively well and might even know some of the children who lived in the area. When Bessie saw Mrs Maguire walking towards her she placed some empty plates she was carrying on an empty table and wiped her hands down the front of her apron. "What can I do you for, miss?" she asked. They sat down together and Mrs Maguire proceeded to tell her story about the children of Dormitory A. Listening intently, Bessie told Mrs Maguire that she herself had left school at fifteen to help her mother run the inn while her father worked in a grocery shop a few streets away. Bessie and her family were well known in the neighbourhood, as was the norm with many business owners in the area. Bessie was very sympathetic. "Don't know if I can help you, miss. I will ask around for you."

Mrs Maguire thanked her for her time and made her way back to her room. David, who was waiting in the foyer, began following her when a voice said, "Why, sir, you can't be going up there. You ain't got a room paid for." It was the old lady who greeted them upon their arrival the previous evening.

"Of course he hasn't," replied Mrs Maguire. "However, this gentleman is my brother and we are looking for his children so if you don't mind we'd like to get on with it."

"Children? What children?" replied the old lady, standing at the bottom of the stairs with her hands on her hips.

"My children," David said sternly as he looked down at the old lady. "And my sister is looking for a number of young children in her care."

"Well, I saw a dozen young'ins not more than two days ago round the back goin' through all the bins. Looking for scraps, they were."

"Really?" asked David enthusiastically. "What happened to them? Where did they go?"

"Shoo'd 'em away, I did. Makin' a big mess outside. Nothin' but trouble."

"It could be them!" Mrs Maguire's face lit up. "We have hope."

"Please," David begged, "if they return, please tell us immediately. Don't tell them to leave, I will personally be responsible for any trouble they cause."

"Well, alright then. I'll be sure to let you know." The old lady walked off, cussing under her breath. She returned to the foyer and regained her position behind the front desk.

"What shall we do now?" Mrs Maguire asked David as they walked down the hallway to her room. David paused in the hallway, thinking. His mind was clouded with questions. *Why did William travel? Is Isabel with him? Are they safe? Do they know I'm still alive?* He just couldn't think straight. He couldn't do much either, having no money to speak of. If it were his children rummaging through the bins behind the inn, they would have done so out of sheer desperation. He deduced they had no money to buy food.

"Well," he responded, "I am going to look for them. I need to know if they are my children."

Mrs Maguire put her room key back in her bag, ready to go with him. David placed his hand on hers and told her to stay in her room, that it was not safe walking the streets at night and she would need to stay behind in case the children returned. In any case, David needed to clear his head. He needed time to think about what he would say to his children if he found them. What would he tell them about his own reason for travelling through the oak tree? Three years is not long in a lifetime, but it is a lifetime to be away from your children. Mrs Maguire was hesitant, but agreed with David and waited in her room. He returned to the lobby and walked out of the front door.

Not knowing exactly where to start, David began with Sussex Gardens and continued straight, turning right at Eastbourne Terrace, alongside the railway station. He walked through alleyways, turning up boxes to see if any of the homeless were Isabel and William. He took particular notice of door thresholds, which might be a place where a child would hide away from the cool night air and away from being seen by dangerous people. After several hours, it was dark and David was tired and hungry. It would have to be the end of today's search, he thought as he began walking back towards the direction of the inn, passing Talbot Square.

Before he re-entered the lobby, he walked around the back, wondering whether the children might have returned in his absence. The laneway was empty except for an old cat who was sound asleep near a pile of rubbish. Its long body curled around, its head tucked comfortably under its paws. David's footsteps woke the sleeping cat and it looked up at David, held its stare then went back to sleep. Perhaps it was too early for the children to return, perhaps they had left the area for good.

David opened the back door and entered the kitchen through the small corridor, which was filled with wooden crates of vegetables and fruit. He expected to see a flurry of activity in the main area of the kitchen; cooks boiling soups and stews over hot stoves, waiters and waitresses collecting meals to and from the dining room, but it was unusually quiet, just some voices from another room. However, as David approached the dining room, the voices grew louder. People were laughing and talking over each other. He continued to walk through the kitchen and opened the doors to the dining room. Sitting on a big armchair in the corner of the room was Mrs Maguire. Twelve children huddled around her. They were all chatting and tucking into tea and scones. They didn't hear David enter, nor did they notice him. They were glad to see Mrs Maguire, who had cared for them for so many years. She was in the midst of telling the children she left the workhouse to look for them and that bad man, Mr Babbage, was gone for good.

During the excitement, Mrs Maguire looked up and noticed David standing in the dining room, just staring at the children. Not staring at all of the children, but two children in particular. There sat Isabel and William on the floor with the other children. When Mrs Maguire stopped talking, all of the children looked around to see what had caught her attention. "It's the man with one hand," came a voice from the group.

"Dad!" said William. His voice quivering. He was stunned.

"Daddy?" said Isabel standing up slowly.

The loud banter that filled the room was now silent. All of the children sat there, not knowing what exactly was going on. Mrs Maguire was even more perplexed. "This man is your father?"

"Oh, Isabel! William!" David ran towards his children. Isabel and William ran through the big room dodging chairs and tables and threw themselves at their father. He wrapped his arms around them and hugged them tightly. For several moments they just stood and held each other.

David stepped back and looked down at his children. How they had grown in three years. William was almost as tall as he and Isabel had lost her little chubby cheeks. She was almost a teenager.

"I can't believe it's you," whispered Isabel.

"We thought you were dead," said William.

"I can't believe it either," replied David as he wrapped his arms around his children once again. "We need to talk. I suppose you have lots of questions that need answering."

"You have no idea," replied William.

Mrs Maguire stood up and walked over to the trio. "David, I had no idea that Isabel and William were *your* children. Did you not know William and Isabel were at the workhouse?"

"Workhouse?" said David. "You were at the workhouse too?"

"We all were," said Isabel. "All twelve of us. We escaped and Mrs Maguire came to London to find us."

"I know," said David. "We came together."

"Oh my gosh," said William. "You're the man who was trying to escape. I saw you but didn't know it was you. Oh, Dad!"

"It's alright, son. You weren't to know. It doesn't matter now that we're finally together."

"Here," said Mrs Maguire, holding out her hand, "take my room key and have some private time together. I'll have tea sent up."

David took the key and mouthed the words 'thank you' to Mrs Maguire. Had it not been for her kindness and generosity, he wouldn't be standing here holding his children once again. Leading his children away, he whispered, "How on earth did you find out about the trees in the park?"

"Rather by accident," said William.

On the way to Mrs Maguire's room William and Isabel told their father everything, right up to their arrival in London. "Then we just hung around this guest house because it was the first place we saw when we got off the train," said Isabel. "Last night we found some used food bags outside the back and the old lady shooed us away."

"Yes, she told me."

"What are you doing in 1851 then?" asked William.

"Ah yes," said David as he sat on the bed. "I went to find a member of our family and bring him home." The children looked perplexed. "You see, our family has a secret. I'm sure you are familiar with Mr Brown, the park caretaker?"

"Oh yes!" cried Isabel. "We found out he's been selling children to the workhouses."

"That's right," replied David. "Well, Mr Brown is your great-uncle and he actually sold his own son. A very evil man indeed."

"Great-uncle!" Isabel and William looked at each other astonished.

"Yes," said David. "His son is Peter Brown and as soon as I found out he had been sold off, I went to find him. Your mother and Mr Brown have been able to travel through the trees for years. She cut all ties with him because she felt they should all leave well alone from the trees but Brown kept going back. It was becoming a dangerous business and she wanted nothing to do with it. And when you two were born, that was the catalyst for staying away from the trees for good. She didn't want you to find about the trees ever."

"Is this why we haven't met Peter?" asked Isabel. "What happened to him?"

"He didn't make it home," said David. "That's how I lost my hand." The children looked at his arm as David covered it under his jacket. "I found Peter and as we were trying to escape, he was dragged under a horse and cart. I tried to save him and the wheel went straight over my wrist. My hand was crushed and so it was amputated."

Isabel threw her arms around her father and cried, "You're still the same, Dad."

William hugged his father. "Yeah, Dad, we don't care what you look like. You're back and that's all that matters."

"Mum told us that you died in a car accident. Why would she do that?" asked Isabel.

"Ah well," replied David. "I can only assume that because I hadn't come back, she must have thought I really did die. You do understand that I can't go home with you."

"Oh, Daddy, but why?" asked Isabel.

"I've changed since being here. I don't have a hand and I need both of my hands on the tree to return."

"Surely something can be done," said William. "We have to get you home where you belong."

"I belong here. This is my life now. I can't change that."

Isabel buried her head in her hands and cried. "Oh, Daddy," she sobbed, "You must come home. We'll work out a way."

William hugged Isabel and assured her that they would find a way to get their dad back home where he belonged. Not only had he felt responsible for Isabel's wellbeing but now he had a much bigger issue to deal with and that was keeping the family together, the whole family. He imagined how wonderful it would be to arrive home together, open their front door, and see the look on their mother's face when she saw her husband standing there with his children. To be home seemed like an impossible feat yet he had to find a way. It was up to him now, he had to make things right again. He had to ensure they would all be together again.

Bessie knocked on the door and brought a tray with tea into the room. "I heard you found each other," she said as she poured the tea. "That's lovely. Here you go now. A nice cup of tea and a slice of cake."

"Thank you," said David.

Bessie left the room and closed the door gently behind her. David, William and Isabel sat together, sipping the warm tea. They didn't have much of an appetite for they knew in their hearts that the children would be returning home without their father. David told the children that he would take them to Bishops Park and say their goodbyes the following day. It was also agreed that the nine children who were also travellers would go with them too so they could return to their families.

That night, David and the children explained to Mrs Maguire about the trees in Bishops Park. She knew that Mr Babbage had acquired the children illegally but had no knowledge of the magic trees. At first she didn't believe them. It wasn't until the children told her about the twenty-first century that she realised they were actually telling the truth. She was flabbergasted when David explained that people flew all over the world in aeroplanes, that people drove around in motor cars, and when William told her all about computers and space travel, well, she had to sit down. It was all too much. Mrs Maguire asked hundreds of questions, such as what types of medicines were used in the future and the names of all Great Britain's prime ministers. She learned that Queen Victoria and Queen Elizabeth II reigned for over sixty years.

David and Mrs Maguire discussed the issue of the remaining three orphans of Dormitory A who were born in the 1840s. As times had changed so greatly over the years, David felt that they would not adjust very well to 2013 and it was agreed that they should remain in 1851. Mrs Maguire felt a duty of care to those children and after all they had been though at the workhouse, she was adamant they would not be sent to an orphanage so she decided to take them with her to Surrey to live with her and her sister. When she asked the children if they would like to go with her, they were thrilled.

"Live on a farm?" asked Maisie. "How delightful. We can milk cows and feed chickens," she screeched.

"Not too much work," replied Mrs Maguire. "You'll need an education first."

The children were excited at the prospect of going to school to learn how to read and write. Arrangements were made and a few days later, Mrs Maguire and her three children boarded a train for Surrey. Prior to their departure, they all said their goodbyes to William and Isabel. Maisie gave Isabel a small locket in the shape of a heart she had been wearing around her neck. "Oh, Maisie," said Isabel. "I can't take this, it belonged to your mother."

"Please, I want you to have it. You saved my life." Tears rolled down Maisie's cheeks as she pulled Isabel close and hugged her.

"Thank you," said Isabel. "I'll treasure it for the rest of my life." She took the locket that was held by a piece of twine, placed it around her neck and tied it in a knot. "I'll buy a gold chain for it when I return home and I'll wear it every day."

CHAPTER 16

After Mrs Maguire and her children left for Surry, the inn returned to its usual routine. Guests came and went, people ate lunch and dinner in the dining hall, the old lady sat at the front desk and rifled through papers, her spectacles perched neatly on the end of her nose. It was quiet again, yet today was a sombre day. It was the last day Isabel and William would have with their father. David chaperoned the rest of the children back to Bishops Park where, upon entering the gates, they spread out and found their trees. Like George Fraser, each child placed their hands on their tree and were gone. They had returned home safely.

David wanted to spend as much time as possible with his children before they returned home. After saying goodbye to the friends they had made in Dormitory A, the children left for the park, knowing that when it was time to return home, their father wouldn't be going with them. It was indeed a very sad time for all and no matter how much they tried to be upbeat, the sadness they felt overcame any happy feeling they had inside them. They found a bench in the park and sat down together. David opened his satchel and pulled out a paper bag filled with food that Bessie had kindly prepared for them. They ate pork pies, pieces of cheese and bread and butter while they talked about home, their mother and what life was like after David had his accident. Isabel talked about her best friend, Jessica, while William told his father that his favourite school subjects were science and history.

As the sun faded and darkness fell, a light wind rustled amongst the leaves in the park. The nearby streets were quiet and once again men in caps climbed ladders to light the street lamps. The children watched a young man walk past them to light the lamps in the park and they knew it was time to go home. David put his arms around his children. "Well," he said in a quiet voice, "it's time." They stood up together and began walking over to the oak tree when they heard footsteps approaching. As they kept walking the footsteps grew louder and more frequent, almost running straight towards them.

"Stop right there!" bellowed a man's voice ever so loudly. David and the children spun around. A tall figure walked briskly towards them. They couldn't make out who was calling them. David took a step forward to get a better look, gently pushing his children behind him to protect them from any potential danger. As the tall figure grew nearer, David could make out sideburns on either side of his face, then a long nose appeared followed by eyes and a beard. When the man caught up to them he stopped right in front of them. David recognised him, the children recognised him. Standing on the path right in front of them was Mr Babbage.

Looking David and the children up and down, he spoke in his usual menacing tone. "Where is Mrs Maguire?" David was speechless, while Isabel and William just stood there, frozen with fear. "Well?" he repeated. "I shall ask you one more time. Where is my niece?"

"Mr Babbage!" replied David. "How did you find us…"

"Oh, never mind about that. You left with Mrs Maguire and I own her. She must return to the workhouse and I have come to collect her."

David, realising that Mr Babbage was just an old bully, replied, "She has gone and we don't know where she is. She left us at an inn in the Marylebone area and we have not seen her since." David then stepped aside, holding his children's hands tightly and began walking away.

Turning around, Mr Babbage thundered, "How dare you walk away from me! You'll pay for this." He fumbled around in his coat pocket. "You dirty peasant!" he roared then pulled out a long silver object with a wooden handle. It was a gun. Not just any gun but the revolver that had gone missing from Samuel Colt's stall at the Great Exhibition. He aimed the gun at Isabel and, without hesitating for a second, David threw himself in front of her. Mr Babbage pulled the trigger and the gun fired with a loud bang. A small puff of smoke lingered where the bullet left the barrel and, in a flash, Mr Babbage was gone.

David fell to the ground and quickly placed his hand over the wound. Isabel and William stood there in shock. Blood leaked from David's chest onto the path and formed a pool around the dying man. "Daddy!" screamed Isabel.

William quickly pulled off his jacket and wrapped it around his father's chest to stop the bleeding. "Hang on, Dad," he cried, "you'll be okay."

"What do we do?" cried Isabel.

"We have to save him. I need to get penicillin or he'll die. I need to go back home so we can save him."

"Please, no!" cried Isabel. "Don't leave us here."

"Isabel, you need to wait here and stem the blood. I'll go to Mum's surgery. You must wait here until I return." William got up and ran off into the night while Isabel stayed behind, holding onto her father's chest.

Looking down at her father, she saw his eyes gradually closing. "Stay with me, Dad," she cried. "Please stay."

David slowly opened his eyes and whispered, "Isabel, my angel. I lo... Love... You".

CHAPTER 17

William opened his eyes and he was back in 2013. He knew it straight away for he could hear cars, trucks and buses roaring down roads in the distance. Time was of the essence and he had no time to stop and be thankful that he made it home safely. He had to save his father's life and nothing was going to stop him. Sprinting out of the park gates, he ran towards the direction of the doctors' surgery where his mother worked in the evenings. Although he hated the fact that his mother had two jobs, he was glad that one of them was at a surgery. He knew the security code to the back door and he kept repeating it out loud so he didn't forget it during the chaos that was going on inside his head. Knowing that the number 22 bus would take him directly to the surgery, he saw one coming and jumped on the back of the old Routemaster as it slowed down amongst the traffic. *Come on, come on*, William thought as the bus carried off down the high street, slowing and stopping to collect more passengers. Thankfully, there weren't many passengers at this time in the evening so the journey didn't take as long as it did when William and Isabel would take the bus to meet their mother for lunch during their school holidays.

After what felt like a lifetime, William finally arrived at the surgery. The two-storey building had cameras fixed to the top of the entrance doors that slid open when a sensor indicated people entering and leaving. William ran around the side of the building and a spotlight lit up when he stood at the back door. He punched in the six digit code and waited for the alarm to disengage. After two small beeping noises the door opened. He didn't know exactly where the medicines were kept but knew that penicillin needed to be stored in a refrigerator so he began with his mother's office, a small room behind the reception desk. William poked around cupboards and pulled out packets of gauze, stuffing them into his trousers. Turning around, he saw a small white fridge next to the bed. It was what he had been looking for. In the fridge several shelves were filled with small glass vials of liquid. Each vial was labelled. He scanned them until he came to a dozen vials with 'Penicillium Chrysogenum' written in black ink. He grabbed all of them, as well as all of the vials of morphine to help ease the excruciating pain in which his father would be in. William grabbed the small plastic bag in the empty bin and filled it with the gauze and the vials and ran out of the room. He made his way down the corridor, opened the back door and ran out, leaving the alarm off and the door wide open.

Running back towards the park, William ran onto the main road. He didn't see the car veering towards him. The headlights shone brightly in William's eyes while the car screeched when the driver slammed on his brakes. The driver wasn't quick enough. The car hit William and he flipped onto the bonnet, coming down onto the ground with a thud. The car stopped in the middle of the road and the driver ran over to William who lay on the road injured. Several cars nearby pulled over and ran to William's aid. One driver pulled out his mobile phone and dialled 999. "Ambulance, please," William heard as he tried to sit up.

"No, no, no! You must stay still," said a woman as she scrunched up a coat and placed it under his head.

"I'm okay," William replied, his voice trembling. "I need to... My dad..." He couldn't put a sentence together yet he had to find the strength to get up and get back to Bishops Park to save his father.

"What's your name?" came another voice.

"William Pritchard."

The driver of the car who hit William bent over him and said, "I'm Paul and I'm a doctor. You'll be okay but we need to get you to a hospital."

"No... Find my dad," stammered William.

"Don't move," said Paul. "We'll call your dad. What's his name?"

How could William explain where his father was? To say he was in Bishops Park was easy enough but in 1851 was something he couldn't possibly explain, or expect anyone to believe. It was no use. His head hurt and he couldn't think properly. He just knew he had to get the medicine to his dad. Remembering how Isabel was alone with him, he began to cry. She would be frightened in the dark. Shortly afterwards, the sound of an ambulance siren grew louder as it approached the scene of the accident and William was gently lifted onto a gurney by two paramedics. Inside the ambulance, a paramedic stuck a drip into his arm while the other paramedic sped off, heading straight for the casualty department.

As William was being wheeled into the hospital, the bright lights on the ceiling flashed past until he was taken into an area and a curtain drawn around him. He felt a searing pain in his left leg and wondered whether it was broken. As the morphine began to take hold, the pain subsided. Fortunately he hadn't lost consciousness so he was still aware of how much time had passed. It must have been about an hour since he left his father so there was a good chance he could still save him. It was still possible; however, if indeed he did have any broken bones, he wouldn't be able to go through the tree. *Think, think*, he thought. His mind was racing with ideas of how he could possibly get back to his father and Isabel. A doctor soon introduced himself and confirmed his leg was broken and he had a mild concussion. Those were his only injuries with the exception of a few cuts and scratches.

A broken leg. The worst possible news in the whole world. There was no way William was able to travel back now. He felt total despair, total helplessness and a complete failure. He was so angry that he foolishly got himself hit by a car. While he lay in casualty, waiting for a nurse to prepare the plaster cast for his leg, his thoughts turned to all of the friends he had made from Dormitory A. He wondered what Mrs Maguire and her children would be doing right now. They would be happy in Surrey, going to school every day, making new friends. Little Maisie would be having a wonderful time feeding chickens and milking cows. What a wonderful life for them after such an awful fate and bleak future in the workhouse. And George Frazer. "George Frazer!" shrieked William as he sat straight up in bed. "George! He's here, in 2013! He made it back!" William couldn't travel back but George could. He could take the medicine back to his father and bring Isabel home. Before they said their goodbyes, George gave William his phone number. So he wouldn't ever lose it, William stuck the tiny piece of paper under the sole of his shoe. "Excuse me," William hollered out.

A nurse entered the room. "What's up honey?" she asked as she propped up his pillow.

"My shoes, where are my shoes?" he said excitedly.

"Right here." She pointed under the bed.

"Please may I have them?" he asked, holding out his arms.

"Oh, well all right," she said as she bent down and picked up his shoes. "Don't suppose you'll be running off with that broken leg of yours," she chuckled.

Before the nurse had even left the room William ripped out the sole in his left shoe and underneath it was a small piece of paper folded up. He opened it up and there was George's number. "Wait!" William said to the nurse. "I'd like to call my parents."

"Of course, honey. Doctor was waiting for you to tell us who your parents were so we can call them. I'll come back with a phone."

The nurse left and returned a few minutes later with a cordless phone. William began dialling. After a few seconds the number began to ring. It rang several times. *Come on*, William thought, *answer it!* The phone went to voicemail where an automated message responded, asking the caller to leave a message. William hung up and dialled again. After a few rings, a voice answered, "Hello?" It was a voice William recognised.

"George! It's William! William Pritchard!"

After a brief silence, George shouted down the phone, "Oh man! Is it really you? Woohoo, you made it back!"

"Yes but under the worst possible circumstances."

William told George everything and when he mentioned that Isabel was still in 1851 with her dying father George jumped at the chance to help. "I'll go back," he said. "I'll do it and I'll bring Isabel home."

Shortly afterwards, George arrived at the hospital and the two boys embraced each other like brothers who hadn't seen each other in decades.

"There's no time to lose," said William as he handed George the bag of medicine. George gave his friend one last hug and ran out of the room and grabbed his scooter at the reception desk.

Weaving past pedestrians, George scooted straight to Bishops Park. The night air was cool and it was completely dark except for the street lights that lit the park entrance. George had made it to the park in record time. He scooted into the park and headed straight for the oak tree. Ensuring the bag of medicine was tied tightly around his waist, he raised both hands and slapped them against the tree. He closed his eyes and waited for the gust of wind that rose up from beneath his feet. It whirred up until it was silent again. Opening his eyes, the park was still dark. The time was exactly the same as it was in 2013 but, once again, it was 1851. George felt nervous about being back. The last time he was in 1851 he was sold to a workhouse and was stuck there for three years. He turned around and a few metres away, near a park bench, saw a small figure crouched over a crumpled heap. It was quiet and there was no movement. George knew it was Isabel. He ran over to her and cried, "Isabel, Isabel, it's me, George."

Isabel was lying over her father, her head resting on his chest. Slowly she raised her head and looked up at George. Her eyes were red and puffy from crying. "George?" she whispered.

"Yes it's me." Kneeling down, he examined David, whose eyes were now closed.

"Where's my brother?"

"I'll explain later. I'm here to help your dad. I've got medicine." Pulling the bag from his belt, George tipped out the contents onto the grass. The little glass bottles clanked together as they fell. Isabel reached her hand across and placed it over George's hand.

"It's too late," she said softly. "He's gone." George checked for a pulse. Nothing. "I can't leave him."

"We have to, Isabel. You need to come back with me. I can't leave you here." Isabel knew George was right. She had to say goodbye to her father, the last time she would ever see him again. She bent down, gently kissed his forehead and slowly stood up. George put his arm around her. "Your brother is fine," he said. "He was hit by a car and has a broken leg so he couldn't come back, which is why I'm here."

"I'm glad he's okay. I guess it's time to leave now." Looking over her shoulder, she looked at her father one last time and walked away.

CHAPTER 18

Isabel and George had safely made it back to 2013. Stepping away from the oak tree, they found the little path and made their way out of the park. Isabel knew that the first thing she had to do was go straight to the hospital to see William and break the news that their father had died. "Come on," said George as he scooped up his scooter. "Hop on and I'll take you to the hospital."

Arriving at the hospital, George whisked Isabel past the reception area and straight through to the emergency department where William was sitting up in bed with his leg propped up with pillows. Isabel heard William's voice and immediately knew which bed he was in. When she found William's bed and pulled back the curtain, a woman quickly turned around. It was Mother. Isabel stood at the door and just stared, shocked to see her mother there with William. Mother threw her arms around her so tightly, Isabel thought she might break. "Oh, Isabel," she said, sobbing. "William told me everything. It's okay, you're home now," she said as she stroked her hair.

"Is Dad okay?" asked William.

Silence filled the room then Isabel burst into tears. George stepped into the room and sat on the bed next to William. "He didn't make it, William. I'm so sorry. I got there as fast as I could and when I found them, he was gone."

"I was too late getting back," William said as he slumped down in the bed. "I didn't do enough." Tears welled up in his eyes. "I'm sorry, Mum."

"Oh, William. It's not your fault, it's not anybody's fault except for that awful man who hurt him."

Mother squeezed William's hand as she looked into his teary eyes. Looking at both her children, she told them they were so heroic for risking their lives to save all those children at the workhouse. She was so proud of them, her heart was bursting. She told William he was such a wonderful brother to ensure Isabel's safety throughout the whole ordeal. Turning to George, she thanked him for compromising his own safety to bring Isabel home. She gave him a big hug and told him he was now a part of their family. George beamed and told her he'd love nothing more than to have a new brother and sister, especially because he didn't have any of his own. He always wanted a little sister and now he had one. That evening, the nurse plastered William's broken leg while Mother brought some sandwiches from the cafeteria. The children hungrily devoured the sandwiches and George left shortly afterwards. He knew he would be seeing a lot more of William and Isabel.

The rest of the evening, Mother, Isabel and William talked about the magic trees in the park. It was true what their father had said about Mr Brown, he did indeed sell his own son to the workhouse and Mother assumed that he had died trying to bring him home. Isabel and Mother left the hospital later that night when a young doctor told them William was being transferred to a children's ward. He would have to stay in hospital for a few days until he was well enough to go home. When William was told the cast would remain on his leg for six weeks he didn't feel upset at the prospect of missing football for the rest of the season. Things had changed now. He had bigger issues on his mind. The loss of his father yet again meant that he and Isabel had to start grieving all over again. However sad he felt, he was glad to have spent just a little more time with him. He had also learnt a lot about himself, that he was strong, wise and brave. He also appreciated his home life, school, his friends and, most of all, his family.

William hardly slept during his first night in hospital. At sixteen, he was considered a minor and was placed in the children's ward. At least the rooms were colourful, with blue skies painted on the ceiling and clowns and fields covering the walls. It was a prettier sight than stark white walls in the adult wards. He didn't mind, for he would be going home in a few days anyway. The ward was silent as the children slept soundly in their beds. His leg felt heavy with the plaster cast wrapped from his ankle to his knee and he kept thinking of his father lying on the grass where he left him in 1851. Knowing that

Mr Babbage had gotten away with murdering his father, he felt the anger at Mr Babbage was building up inside him. *He must pay,* he thought. *He must be brought to justice. He will pay for taking my father.*

CHAPTER 19

Mrs Maguire, Maisie, Tommy and Albert arrived safely in Surrey. Excitedly, the children jumped onto the platform when the train came to a screeching halt. Carriage doors opened and the platform was a flurry of activity with mothers, fathers and children, porters stacking big brown suitcases on trolleys for the first class passengers, all making their way out of the narrow gates and off in different directions. Horses and carriages waited as they filled up with commuters, then galloped away, kicking up dust with their hooves. As the station emptied out, standing at the end of the platform was a young woman. She wore a long cream dress to her ankles with black boots. A yellow bonnet was tied under her chin and curls of dark hair hung down her back. When she saw Mrs Maguire she waved her arm and walked briskly towards the group. "Sister!" she hollered. After embracing each other she looked at the children and held out her hand to greet them. "Well, you must be Tommy," she said to the youngest boy.

"I am, miss," he replied as he shook her hand.

"And you're Albert."

"Yes, miss," said Albert taking his cap off his head.

Turning to a blushing Maisie, she said, "And, my dear, you must be none other than Maisie." Maisie, being a shy child, didn't respond. Instead she stood behind Mrs Maguire. "Well then. My name is Miss Lowood but as we are all friends you must call me Mabel."

"Yes, Miss Mabel," the children responded.

"Just Mabel." She winked.

After a brief chat the group left the station and walked down a small path for a mile and a half until they arrived at her small cottage. Along the way they chatted merrily, Miss Lowood telling the children about her little cottage and all the animals that she lived with. There were twenty-two chickens, including four roosters, three goats, several cats who had made her small couch their sleeping quarters, fifteen cows that lived in a large shed at the back of the farm and a few mice that Miss Lowood was very keen to get rid of. Unfortunately the cats were quite old and couldn't keep up with the speed at which the mice ran so the mice had to stay. Tommy informed Miss Lowood that he had caught a few mice at the workhouse and he was actually pretty good at setting traps. Miss Lowood was delighted.

When the children arrived, Miss Lowood made tea and served a sponge cake she had baked that morning. They all sat around the small table in the kitchen and ate together. Maisie wiped her mouth on the hem of her dress. "Ah," said Miss Lowood, "clothes aren't for wiping mouths on." Maisie looked up at her sheepishly and waited for a telling off. "They're for getting dirty outside," said Miss Lowood as she winked at Maisie. Maisie began chuckling, as did Miss Lowood. Her laugh was infectious and so everybody began laughing. Albert wasn't quite sure what everyone was laughing at, but he felt happy and laughed anyway.

Later that evening, the children washed and wearily climbed into bed. Miss Lowood had converted the attic into their bedroom which had three beds with a chest at the end of each bed for the children's clothes. A small bookcase sat under the window with several books she had kept from her own childhood. She planned to help the children learn to read and write before they began attending school. For now, they would settle in and help out on the farm. Tommy and Albert would milk the cows while Maisie collected the chickens eggs and help out inside the cottage. She cooked meals, baked cakes and scones and, during the quieter times of the day, helped Miss Lowood and Mrs Maguire wash clothes in a shed around the side of the cottage. After dinner each night, the children sat by the fire while Miss Lowood read stories. She loved having the children around. She didn't have a husband nor did she expect to find one living on the outskirts of a small village in Surrey. The village was a ten minute walk from the cottage and consisted of a shop where one could buy bread, milk and groceries, a grain store, and a small church at the end of the narrow road which had a small school at the back where children from nearby farms would walk to and attend class. With three new children attending, the school would soon have eighteen, ranging from the ages of seven to thirteen. At fourteen, the children would finish their education and either work on their family farm or exceptionally bright boys would wait another two years and attend university.

On their first day of school, the children woke excitedly. They each took turns washing their faces in a small basin. They brushed their hair and dressed in smart looking clothes Mrs Maguire had bought them. They wore brand new boots and helped each other tie up the laces. After bread with butter and jam for breakfast they walked to school together, accompanied by Miss Lowood and Mrs Maguire. On the way, Miss Lowood gave them spelling tests of words they had learned over the past week. "Spell 'tree'," she said to Maisie.

"T-R-E-E."

"Oh, well done!"

"Tommy. Spell 'grass'."

"G-R-A-S-S," replied Tommy.

"Excellent."

"And Albert. Spell 'hearth'."

Stuttering, Tommy finally got the words out "H-A-R... Oh wait... I know it... H-E-A-R-T-H."

"Well done, Albert. Well done." The children clapped their hands. Beaming proudly, Albert held his head high as he walked along. As the youngest of the children, Albert found learning a little more difficult than Tommy and Maisie. At school, the children were introduced to their new teacher, an older woman called Mrs Peters. She was married to the owner of the grain store and together they had two grown up children who had moved away from Surrey to live in London. The school consisted of two rooms, the larger one for the children that had three rows of desks, one for each child, and another room as Mrs Peters' office.

The children settled into school well. They made friends with the other children and enjoyed school life. In particular, it was Maisie who flourished. Her shyness waned and she became quite popular with her classmates as her generous nature and loving personality warmed her to everyone she met. She often shared her lunch with other children who did not have as much to eat and as her reading skills improved, she was able to help Albert with his. They became quite close, even referring to each other as brother and sister. Mrs Maguire found work at the grocery store which meant she didn't have to dip into her savings, for she wanted to save enough money to buy a home for herself and the children.

CHAPTER 20

After a three-day stay in hospital, William returned home to Windermere Drive. Six weeks later, the plaster was removed and the crutches were returned to the hospital. For a few days his leg was white and pasty from the plaster and Isabel teased him about his two different coloured legs. He and Isabel stayed away from Bishops Park and George Fraser became a regular visitor at the house. The children spent most of their time talking about their travel through the trees. It was surreal and they still couldn't believe all of the events that had taken place over the past few months. Life went on, however, things had not returned to normal for they now knew that their father had been alive for the past three years, while previously thinking he had died in a car accident. Now they knew that he was dead – killed by Mr Babbage. William couldn't get the image of his father lying helplessly on the grass out of his mind. He felt guilty that he had to leave him there, that he couldn't give him a proper burial, that he couldn't bring him home, whether it be dead or alive. Mother was also different. The sadness etched on her face every time she came home from work was obvious. She tried her best to remain upbeat for the sake of her children but William saw right through it. One evening, William heard his mother's car pull up in the driveway. After expecting her to walk through the door a few minutes later, he looked out of the front window and saw her sitting in the car, crying. She wiped her puffy eyes in the rear view mirror, patted her red cheeks and took a deep breath. When she walked through the front door she was smiling and told her children what a lovely day she had.

Isabel and William's mother was born Elinor Jane Brown. She met David when they were at high school. Elinor studied politics and was the only girl in the class so she felt like an outcast from her first day at school. None of the boys wanted to sit near her. She wasn't pretty like many of the other girls. She felt awkward being tall and skinny. Her oversized school uniform hung down below her knees, freckles covered her nose and spread out over her cheeks and her mousey brown hair hung past her shoulders. She was also shy which proved difficult when it came to making friends. On the other hand, David was popular. He had lots of friends and everyone at school knew him. He was athletic and his muscular legs, broad shoulders, deep blue eyes and witty sense of humour attracted the attention of many girls at school. He was captain of both the swimming and cricket teams. He also got along well with the teachers as he was clever and often challenged them in class, asking all sorts of interesting questions which gave rise to some very interesting debates.

David first noticed Elinor on their first day of class. Being the only girl, it was hard not to notice her sitting in the front row all by herself. David usually sat in the middle row with his best friend, Charles, while the other boys spread themselves around the room. While David and Elinor never spoke to each other outside class, David would be courteous to Elinor every time they engaged in classroom discussions. One particular morning, the class were discussing what level of power a judge has in a courtroom. David argued that a judge should have the power to overturn a guilty verdict while Elinor argued that the jury should remain the decision makers based on the facts of the case. As they both put forward their arguments, David realised that this tall, lanky, mousey brown-haired girl was actually a really smart and interesting person. She was just as good at presenting an argument as him and he found this fascinating. By the time class had finished, he was smitten and wanted to ask her out for a coffee after school. Did she even drink coffee? More to the point, did she even like David? For the first time in his life, David felt a shyness he hadn't experienced before and realised this is how she must feel every single day. He began to understand her. It took two weeks until he felt courageous enough to speak to Elinor outside the classroom. So, one afternoon after class, he followed her to her locker. Walking behind her, dodging students walking through the corridors, she arrived at her locker, pulled out a key from her coat pocket and opened it. As she rummaged around, pulling at books and folders she picked up a large maths book and dropped it into her bag on the floor. Slamming her locker shut there was David, standing, looking like a little boy who dropped his ice cream into his lap.

After a few seconds of silence, she spoke. "Can I help you?"

"Um... Well... Actually, yes," David responded. "I really enjoyed your argument you made in class about juries and their level of power in the courtroom."

Elinor thought this was a little weird. First of all, the most popular boy in the school was talking to her and secondly, that he was interested in her views. "Really?" she mused. "Well I thought your debate was interesting too."

David felt a little relaxed after hearing this. He felt the confidence returning. "Would you like to go for a coffee one afternoon after school? We could check out that new coffee shop on"

"I'd love to!" Elinor squealed before David could finish his sentence.

"Excellent. How about Thursday?"

"Sure."

And that was it. David and Elinor fell in love on their first date at The Gleaming Bean coffee shop and they became inseparable ever since. They sat in politics class together in the middle row with Charles, who also really liked Elinor. On summer weekends, Elinor watched David play cricket and during the winter she occasionally attended his swimming trials. Most of his swimming training began at 6am but she wasn't about to get out of bed in the freezing cold for that! David would tease her about not being a 'proper' girlfriend in supporting him at swimming training and she teased him back by telling him that she was far cleverer because she got an A+ for her midterm exams, while he only achieved an A-!

After graduating from high school, David studied medicine and several years later became a doctor, while Elinor studied nursing. David wanted to help as many people as possible so, after getting married, they flew to Africa and spent five years helping the sick in poor villages. As soon as Elinor found out she was having a baby, they decided that the best place for their child to grow up would be at home, back in London. Shortly afterwards, William was born. Life was happy and became even lovelier when they welcomed a baby girl who they named Isabel. William adored his little sister. He was four when she was born and was happy to help his mother change nappies and feed his little sister her milk. Sometimes he thought she was a bit boring when she spent most of the day sleeping. He just wanted her to grow up and start talking so they could be pirates together and play with cars and trains. No, she wouldn't be playing with dolls like other little girls. Isabel would do just as her big brother would. And that's the way it was. By the time Isabel was two, she had quite a collection of toy cars and after school William would set up long lines of tracks in the lounge room and the two of them would race their cars alongside each other. And when they were finished playing with the cars, they would run outside the back to play, leaving a huge mess for Mother to tidy up. "We need a bigger house," she muttered to herself every time the children left a mess of cars and trucks all over the floor.

By the time William started high school, he had become interested in sports and computers. He often had friends over and they played all sorts of computer games in his bedroom. Gradually, Isabel began feeling left out. For so many years, she and William were close, the very best of friends, yet they grew apart as they got older and when their mother came home one evening and sat them down, they knew she was about to tell them some bad news. The news that their father had died shattered their world and they became more or less strangers living in the same house. William became reclusive, spending much of his time in his bedroom on his own, buried in his books. Isabel was alone because Mother now had to work days and most evenings to support the family. William thought she worked long hours so she didn't have to think about Dad or come home to a place that once was filled with laughter but was now filled with sadness.

CHAPTER 21

Several months had passed since the children returned home from 1851. Winter was setting in and the days were getting shorter and colder. William resumed playing football for the school team after his leg had completely healed. In class, Isabel sat next to Jess as she always did. She didn't tell Jess about the magic trees for she knew Jess wouldn't believe her. Looking back, it all seemed so ridiculous. It was a secret which had to be kept within the family.

One evening after dinner, George Fraser arrived at the house. Mother was surprised as William made no mention of George's visit during dinner. George seemed uneasy, nervous, as did William. "I have something to tell you," William said to Mother.

"Oh dear," replied Mother. "What have you done? Have you been expelled at school?"

"No, Mum, it's nothing like that."

"Well then, what is it?"

"Maybe it's better if I give you this to help explain," replied William. He held out his hand and opened it. There in the palm of his hand was the shiny gold fob watch his father had rescued from the floor at the Great Exhibition.

Mother stared at it in amazement. She picked it up and turned it over and read the inscription. Looking at William, she said, "I don't understand."

"We're going back," said William.

"Back where?" Mother knew what William was about to say but didn't want to believe it.

"I need to know what happened to Dad and George is coming with me."

"But, darling, you know what happened."

"Yes. He died. We know that. I just can't live my life wondering what happened to him after we left him in the park."

"Please don't go," begged Mother. "It's too dangerous. I almost lost you and Isabel. We need to move on now."

"I've made up my mind, Mum. George is here because he's coming with me."

"Oh, George," said Mother. "Are you really going too? You don't have to go. You don't have to risk your life for our family."

"I want to go," replied George. "It was William who saved me from the workhouse and brought me back home. It's the least I can do."

"Well, knowing William, there's no way I can change his mind," said Mother. "All I can say is stay safe. I guess things might be easier this time because you've been there before, so you'll know what to expect."

It was agreed that Isabel would stay behind with Mother. She was still traumatised after seeing her father pass away. Plans were made, and the following week William and George left the house on Windermere Drive and headed for the park. This time things would be different, life would change for someone. William was going to bring Mr Babbage to justice. It was time to finally confront him.

CHAPTER 22

When the boys arrived back in 1851, William stood at the exact spot where his father had died. All that was left was a patch of grass. It was as though his father had never existed, never been to 1851, never been to Bishops Park. He may have been erased from history but he would never be erased from William's memory. George stood at the oak tree and waited for William. He knew this would be a sad journey, a journey of mixed emotions to find out what happened to William's father.

However sad he felt, William was ready. He decided their first stop was to find any records of where his father might be buried so they headed for the library, the same library where he and Isabel found out about the history of the park. The brick building looked the same as it always did over the years. Not much had changed on the outside. Inside, however, the library was vastly different. All of the metal shelving was gone; instead books sat on wooden shelves around the perimeter of the walls. To the rear, a wrought iron staircase spiralled up and around to the top floor where more books sat on dusty shelves. The floor was bare wood, there was no carpet and it felt cold and looked lifeless. In the middle of the room was a big desk covered with newspapers. William walked over to the desk and picked up the *London Evening Standard*. The date was 3 November 1851. As William and George looked around the big room, an old man appeared from a door at the side of the building. His wiry grey hair hung below his ears where more tuffs of grey hair grew from within his ears. It was hard to see where the hair from his head stopped and the hair in his ears began. His back was hunched over and he propped himself up with a walking stick. He didn't seem to notice William and George standing at the newspaper desk. He slowly shuffled along to the other side of the room dragging his feet with each step. William followed. "Excuse me, sir."

The old man stopped and turned around. Looking William up and down he responded, "Yes, what is it? What do you want?" The old man's eyes were dark. The skin covering his face was wrinkled and his nose was red and blotchy. He smelt like a pile of old clothes that had been sitting on the floor for a very long time.

"I'm looking for some records of any deaths in the past six months or so. Can you help us?"

The old man looked over towards George which made him feel quite uncomfortable. "I can't help you," he snapped and shuffled away. William sighed, his shoulders shrank as he stood watching the old man disappear again.

"Come on," said George. "We'll find him, don't worry. We didn't come this far to get beaten by an old grump."

"You're right. I guess we should expect this kind of attitude. I mean, nobody knows us and to an adult, we must look like a couple of silly runaways."

Scanning the room, William noticed a door on the opposite side of the library. "Let's see what's over there," he said. The door was open so the boys let themselves in. The room was dark with only a small window at the rear. Shelves were packed with books, not reading books but record books.

"This is it!" exclaimed George. "This must be where they keep all the records."

"Well then, why don't you start by checking out those books over to that side of the room and I'll start on this side. Hopefully we'll find something relevant."

The boys poured through the books. The first column had the date, the second had the first and surnames of various people and the third column contained a brief description of how that person died. Many people died of tuberculosis and pneumonia, while others died of typhoid. It saddened William to see that so many of the names were those of children. 'Killed under horse and cart' read one entry. 'Unknown' read another with an empty space in the date of death column.

Eventually George found a dozen books bound together with dates ranging from January to October 1851. "This is it!" he shouted. "Here. Start on these and I'll go through the rest." He carried half a dozen books over to William who was sitting on the floor amongst piles of record books and plonked them in front of him. The boys read every single entry but David's name was nowhere to be found. They took particular attention to the 'Unknown' entries where a name should have appeared. They didn't see any description of a man without a hand or a man found in a park who died of a gunshot wound. They couldn't find anything at all even remotely resembling William's father.

"Well then," said William, looking around the room, dismayed, "we've searched all of these records."

"Maybe we start looking in local graveyards," suggested George.

"Perhaps. Although if someone has been buried then there would be a record. And that record should be in this room. I just don't get it."

"Maybe the records aren't accurate," replied George. "I mean, we don't know who wrote these entries. Maybe they didn't do their job properly. They could have had kids write these entries. If it's okay for us to slave away in a workhouse then surely this kind of work could be done by a child."

"I guess so," agreed William. "We have to keep thinking this is 1851 not 2013. The way of life is very different here. We have to stop thinking like our normal selves and start thinking like the nineteenth century way of life."

"What do we do now?"

William looked sternly at George. "I'm sorry, George, but there's another reason why I wanted to come back."

George, detecting the graveness of William's voice, sat down next to William. "All right, let's have it."

"I want to confront Babbage. I don't know what I'll do when I see him, but I need to confront the man who killed my father."

"Are you sure that's wise? I mean, how will you react if you do see him? What if he still has the gun?"

"I've thought of that," replied William. "But I can't let it go. He can't get away with it. You can't just kill someone and walk away."

"But, Will, finding Babbage and confronting him will be dangerous. He's a dangerous man."

"I know but what he did to my dad was the worst thing you can do to a human being. My father was a good man. He was a doctor who helped hundreds of people. He saved lives. He and Mum spent time in

Africa going around villages helping the sick. They chose that life. They could have just had comfortable jobs in a hospital where you can go home to a nice house every night. In Africa they slept in huts and worked tirelessly to help others. My dad deserves justice as well as a proper burial."

"Gosh, Will, I didn't realise you felt so strongly about it. Well, mate, whatever you do I'm with you. We're brothers after all."

"Thanks, brother," replied William. "Don't think I could do any of this without you." After a brief pause, William continued, "You know, George, I'd really like to find Mrs Maguire and see how Maisie, Tommy and Albert are getting on. But first things first, we need to find Babbage."

"Let's do it," replied George. "Let's get it over with."

William and George decided to stay at the Marylebone inn where they had previously stayed with Mrs Maguire, their father and the children of Dormitory A. It was a place they were familiar with so they made their way over to the inn, hitching a lift on the back of a horse and cart, unbeknownst to its driver. When they arrived the little old lady at the front desk was still there, as was Bessie who was waiting on tables. When she saw the boys walking past the dining room into the parlour, her eyes lit up. "Hello again," she said, beaming. The boys greeted her with a handshake and she ushered them to sit down on a sofa. "What news?" she asked. "I trust you have returned in good spirits?"

"We are well," replied William. "We just need a room for the night." William didn't want to give too much away so he kept his answers short and to the point.

"Well, I will be happy to oblige. As winter is nearly upon us, trade is slow so most of our rooms are available. I'll tell Mrs McGovern at front desk that you'll be needing two rooms. One for each of you. And don't worry," she whispered, "I'll see to it that you are only charged for one."

Bessie returned with two keys and a tray of tea and scones. The boys tucked into the warm and fluffy scones and invited Bessie to eat with them. As they ate, they chatted about Bessie's life. She told the boys she finished school when she was fourteen so she could help her mother run the inn. She said that Mrs McGovern was her grandmother and it was her great-grandparents who opened the inn over sixty years ago. In those days, the inn was used as a stopover for overnight travellers but nowadays people liked to come to the inn for lunch and dinner. Some of their guests even came quite regularly to sit in the parlour and have tea. She thought that was quite odd considering they had their own homes to have tea but nowadays people liked to be more sociable. She said many of their guests were ladies who liked to sit around and gossip to one another. Much of this year's talk was about the Great Exhibition. Everybody was talking about it. During the six months it was open, it was the talking point of not just London, but the entire country. The guests gushed about the Great Exhibition so much that she felt she had been there herself. After tea, the boys said their goodnights and went to bed early. They were tired and needed to be well-rested for their journey back to Bristol the following day.

Next morning, William and George waited patiently at Marleybone station for the 8.15 train to Bristol. The sky was grey, dark clouds hung over the city and the cold wind blew into the station platforms. The big steam train chugged into the platform, big puffs of steam spewed from the chimney, slowing down until it came to a screeching halt, finally stopping at the barrier. Carriage doors opened, people hopped down onto the platform and walked briskly into the station and disappeared into the streets of London. The freezing cold boys wasted no time and boarded the train out of the chilly morning air, found a seat next to a window and sat opposite each other.

William felt very nervous and uneasy and by the time the train arrived at Bristol Temple Meads, he felt utterly sick. The nausea slowly crept up on him as the train pulled into each station. The palms of his hands were clammy and by the time they finally reached the big iron gates at the workhouse, he felt as though his knees would give way. He stopped just shy of the gates and held his stomach. "Are you all right?" asked George.

"I didn't think this would be so hard," William replied. "For months all I've wanted to do is look this man in the face and bring him to justice, but I just thought I'd be more prepared."

"Well, I guess being back here also brings bad memories. It does for me. I feel awful too."

"Let's do this," said William. "Let's just get it over with."

The boys had spent most of the train journey discussing how they would confront Mr Babbage and have him brought to justice. George thought they should just walk straight into his office and hold him down while the police were called. He would be so surprised to see them that he wouldn't have any time get away. William wanted to grab him and hurt him, just like Mr Babbage hurt his father, but knew this was not the right way of going about it. He wanted Mr Babbage to spend the rest of his life in a prison cell. In any case, if Mr Babbage was indeed hurt in any way by William and George, there might be witnesses and they wouldn't make it back to the station. They would never make it back to London and they would certainly never make it back through the trees. As dusk was already approaching, William suggested they wait until night time so that nobody would see them creeping around in the dark. They were familiar with the routine at the workhouse and knew that after dinner Mr Babbage would be alone in his rooms and the staff and workers would be in theirs.

The boys waited at the front gates and snuck in when the wintery sun began to set. Creeping around the back of the building, they waited until the big wooden door to the kitchen opened to allow two men to haul barrels outside to a nearby shed. They quickly darted through the kitchen door. The kitchen was empty but the aroma of the evening's dinner was still in the air. On the edge of the big table in the middle of the kitchen sat a basket full of bread rolls. The boys filled their pockets. George took a huge bite of bread, crunching on it, crumbs falling onto the floor, as they made their way through the kitchen and down a long hallway until they found themselves in the foyer. When Mr Babbage's door was in full view, the boys looked at each other nervously. William looked around to ensure the coast was clear. "Right then, let's do this," whispered George.

The boys walked slowly and quietly around the perimeter of the big foyer until they reached Mr Babbage's door. William felt as if his heart was going to leap right out of his chest and figured George must be feeling just as nervous. So much was at stake and the boys were well aware of the consequences if they were caught. William raised his hand and knocked on the door. There was no answer. The boys glanced at each other. George nodded his head as a gesture for William to knock a second time. This time William knocked a little harder. Pressing his ear to the door there was nothing but silence. "Open it," whispered George. William turned the handle and opened the door a few centimetres, just enough to determine whether Mr Babbage was actually in the room. Through the tiny gap all he could see was a small section of the fireplace. It was lit and embers cracked and hissed among the bright orange flames. William opened the door further and saw Mr Babbage lying on his bed. He was facing the wall with his back to the door. It seemed odd that Mr Babbage didn't turn around. In fact, he didn't move at all. William thought he must be asleep.

"Stay here," he whispered as he entered the room. George did just that and waited at the door, looking around to see if anyone was coming.

William tip-toed right up to Mr Babbage. Still no movement from the old man so he leaned over towards his face to see if he was in fact sleeping. Under the old man's head on the crisp white pillowcase was a big red stain. It ran from his temple down his cheek and stained a large section of the pillow. His eyes were open. William bent over and noticed a small hole in his head. Looking at the lifeless body, it was clear that the old man was dead. "Oh my..." William said, putting his hand over his mouth. He couldn't even finish his sentence. He was in complete shock.

"What is it?" asked George as he walked over to the bed. When George saw Mr Babbage lying dead on his bed all he could do was gasp. He was too shocked to say anything.

Eventually finding his voice, William declared, "He's dead." Panicked and shaken, the boys spun around and ran. They ran through the kitchen and out of the back doors. They ran all the way out of the big iron gates and onto the dirt road until they were well out of sight of the workhouse.

Stopping for a break, puffing and panting, George said, "Looks like he's been shot. Who though? Who would do it?"

"Everyone and anyone," replied William. "There's a thousand reasons right behind us in that building."

"I just can't believe it."

"I'm glad," said William. "He deserved it. I would love to have done it myself but that's not the right way to deal with it. I would have been happy reporting him to the police but now I realise trying to convince the police he's a murderer when dad's body is nowhere to be found would have been impossible. Now we can head back to London and concentrate on finding my dad."

Walking back to the station, the boys talked only of Mr Babbage's death. They agreed that the person responsible would have entered his room some time after dinner that evening otherwise he would have been missed and the workhouse staff would be looking for him. At dinner he was always seen hovering around the workers, correcting their table manners and generally standing around, looking down at everyone, making sure they were not being served any more food than their rations. Just his presence let everyone know that he was the boss and no one was to put a foot out of line.

The last train had indeed been and gone so the boys found a small stable near the train station where they slept on the hay in an empty stall. They had a small amount of money which they agreed to save for food and emergencies. They slept quite comfortably and were warm after finding several horse blankets hanging over a nearby stall. The next morning they were woken by the sound of horses neighing and moving around, the clip-clopping of their hooves, and horses chomping on grain in buckets that hung from the doors.

"Well that was a first," said George as he yawned and stretched his arms high into the air.

"We were lucky to find this place," replied William. "Last night was cold. At least the horses kept us company," he mused.

"I still can't believe Babbage is dead," said George.

"I just can't imagine who would have done it. I mean, everyone hated him but who in the workhouse would have access to a gun? It just seems impossible."

"You're right. It must have been an outsider," agreed George.

"Right. Well let's head back to London and start looking for that evidence of what happened to Dad."

The boys rolled up the blankets and hung them back over the stable doors and left, patting the horses on the way out. At the train station they found a small food stall and ate bread and butter and drank a hot cup of tea before boarding their train which was already waiting on the platform. As the two finished breakfast they noticed a commotion. A group of men entered the station and began spreading out. Some of the men went straight for the platforms, walking up and down peering into train carriages that were ready to depart. William and George watched and soon realised the men were, in fact, police. They wore long dark blue coats with a row of silver buttons down the front. A thick belt with a big silver buckle sat firmly around their waste while their black trousers hung neatly over their big black boots. People stopped and stared at all the officers. "Over there!" bellowed a young officer as he pointed to the two boys who had just stood up to board their train for London. All of a sudden there was a rush of police running towards William and George. "That's them! They were the ones who did it!"

"Run!" shouted William. Before George could say anything, he found himself running with William onto the nearest platform. They ran all the way down the end until they were stopped by a wire gate which was locked with a big chain and padlock. They were stuck. The gate was too high to climb over and, looking back up the platform, a dozen officers ran towards them.

"What do we do?" yelled George.

"Onto the tracks," said William as he jumped off the platform. "Grab my hand." George grabbed his hand and jumped.

"Murderers!" yelled an officer waving his baton in the air.

"Catch them!" yelled another, but the boys were too fast. They disappeared out of sight, leaving the policemen at the gate fumbling through a bunch of keys trying to find the right one. By the time they had the gate open the boys were gone.

CHAPTER 23

"Why are they after us?" asked George after the boys found an alleyway in which to hide themselves.

"They think we killed Babbage. Someone must have seen us leave his room and put two and two together."

"We can't go back to the station then. The police are everywhere."

"We can't get caught, George. They'll lock us up forever and then we'll be stuck here in 1851."

"I can't bear to think about it," replied George. "Well, if we can't go back to the station how do we get back to London?"

"The same way we got to London when we escaped the workhouse."

Suddenly the boys had several problems on their hands: avoiding capture for a crime they didn't commit, getting back to London and finding William's father. The ensuing days would be an enormous challenge and they knew it. Police would be looking for them all over Bristol so they had to get out of the city as quickly as possible. It was still morning so they waited until later that evening before they could find someone who could help them return to London. Being unfamiliar with the city, the only way they really knew how to get back to London was to return to the workhouse and hide on the wagons that came and went. That option was definitely out of the question. If there were a dozen police at the station then there would be even more police at the workhouse. No, they had to think of another way. A safer way. From their stay at the Marylebone inn, they knew that the inns were frequented by travellers making their way up and down the country by coach. They figured someone might give them a ride towards London, if they paid them a couple of shillings, so they walked down several of the smaller streets of town looking for an inn until they came across the Cloak and Dagger. They were relieved to see a sign on the door that said 'Coaching Inn'.

The inn was filled with groups of men sitting at long wooden benches, their tin cups filled with frothy beer. They chatted loudly amongst themselves while several waitresses walked around the room, refilling their jugs. Some men sat alone eating their meals, others sat in chairs around the fireplace, catching up on sleep before their long journey ahead. William found a small table in the corner and a waitress at the bar approached the table. "What will yers be wantin'?" she asked.

"Actually," said William, "we need to get to London tonight. Do you know anyone who could take us?"

"Well, that man over there," said the waitress, pointing to an older gentleman sitting in the corner on his own. "That's Mr Channing. He goes to London twice weekly."

"Do you think he would take us?" asked William excitedly.

"You'll have to ask him yerself." The waitress bent down and whispered, "Don't much like your chances, though. Most of the goods he takes to London are 'misappropriated', if you know what I mean. Now what will it be, fellas? You can't be using up our tables if you don't order nothin'." A quick glance at the menu and the boys decided on pork pies. "Ale or brandy?"

George giggled when he realised the waitress was offering them alcohol. "We're fine, thanks," replied William. "Just the pies will be enough."

The waitress disappeared while the boys studied Mr Channing sitting on his own, sipping his brandy. Next to his chair was a small round table with an empty plate, knife and fork. "Looks like he's already had his dinner," whispered George. "How do we approach him?"

"Let's wait until he leaves. We can follow him outside and ask him then. If we're seen in here, we might get caught. Who knows, there might even be police in here."

"Good thinking."

A short time later the waitress returned with two pork pies and the boys tucked into them hungrily. Crunching on the warm pies, they ate in silence. Just as William was finishing his meal, he noticed Mr Channing stand up and put on a big coat that was hanging over his chair. "Look. He's leaving."

George stuffed the remainder of his pie into his mouth and began chomping furiously. His mouth was so full of food he couldn't speak so he pointed to the door.

They watched Mr Channing slowly make his way to the front door, his heavy boots pounding on the bare floorboards. He gave the front door a big push and a gush of cold air filled the foyer. The boys left the money for their meal on the table and followed the man outside who was walking towards a big stage coach and four waiting horses. Long brown leather straps bound the horses together. They looped back towards the driver's seat, forming the reins. The big man pulled himself up onto the seat at the front of the coach. When he sat down, the carriage bounced up and down on the big springs that sat above the wheels.

"Excuse me, sir," said William as he approached the coach.

The man looked down at the teenagers. "What do you want?" His voice was deep and menacing.

"We need to get to London. Are you going in that direction?"

The man looked the boys up and down and wondered why two young boys would be travelling so far on their own. "No room," he responded sharply.

"But your coach is empty," said George as he peered into the small windows.

The man bent down to George. "Quite rightly. It is empty but not for long. In the morning the coach will be full by the time I leave Bristol. So, if yer don't mind, be out of me way before you get caught under foot of me 'orses."

Stepping forward, William held out a few shillings. "We have money to pay you and we'd be really grateful. We can even help you with your deliveries, if you'd be so kind as to accept our offer."

The man paused and looked at the shiny coins in William's hand. "Well then," he said, "coach leaves at 7am. I'll no wait for no one." With that the man scooped up the money from William's hand and shoved it in his pocket. "You'll 'ave to sit up 'ere with me but I warn ye, it gets cold up 'ere, it does." The boys thanked Mr Channing and spent the night at The Cloak and Dagger. When they returned to the coach the next morning, Mr Channing was nowhere to be seen. The boys waited nervously when, ten minutes later, the coach door opened and out tumbled Mr Channing. "Well," he said to the waiting boys, "tis me home away from home." He had slept inside the coach the whole night.

After making several stops, the coach was on its way. The horses thundered out of Bristol at full speed. The air was cold and dust kicked up by the horses flew everywhere. Mr Channing gripped the reigns tightly with his big leather gloves. William and George sat in silence. It would be a whole day before they would reach London. Or so they thought.

CHAPTER 24

As the horses galloped away and roared down the dirt highway, Mr Channing spotted something up ahead. Pulling back the reigns to signal his horses to slow down, an outline in the distance became clearer. Three horses with their riders stood in the middle of the road, blocking the way for the coach to pass.

"Oh blazes," Mr Channing cursed.

"What is it?" asked William.

"Robbers," he replied.

"Yield!" yelled one of the men as he waved a large gun in the air.

The coach slowed down and stopped in front of the three men. One of the men climbed down from his horse and walked over to the coach while the others remained on their horses, holding their guns tightly across their chests.

"Just mail for London," said Mr Channing. "No valuables in 'ere."

"Oh, but you do have valuables," said the man. "And they be your companions."

"What do you mean?" asked Mr Channing, looking at the boys sitting next to him. "They just be needing passage to London. Now if yer don't mind we'll be getting on..."

"Stop! Do not move or I will shoot," said the man. "Those boys are wanted for murder."

"Murder!" exclaimed Mr Channing. "It cannot be. Why, they're only children."

"They committed an act of murder at the Bristol workhouse and we have been employed to find them and bring them back to face justice."

"Oh, Mr Channing," interrupted a panicked William. "We didn't do it. When we got there the old man was already dead. We got scared and ran and now we're being blamed for it."

"Please help us," pleaded George.

"There's nothing I can do," said Mr Channing. "I'd like to help but I can't. See they have guns and I'm not ready to meet with me lord just yet. Don't think me wife would like it either. Sorry, lads."

The boys were duly ordered off the coach and returned to Bristol where they were delivered straight to the police station. Inside they were taken into a small cell with one bed, a pillow and blanket. A young policeman locked the cell door with a big brass key that hung on a large bronze ring with a dozen other keys. He placed the bunch of keys on a hook on the opposite side of the room and disappeared. William sat down on the bed, put his hands over his face and let out an almighty sigh. It was the worst possible thing that could have happened to them. How on earth would they get out of this mess now? Finding his father now seemed like an impossibility. It was an absolute nightmare.

Seeing the anguish on William's face, George gave him a much-needed hug. "We'll get out. We'll be all right. We didn't do anything wrong and we will prove it in court."

"Court!" William replied. "Do you know how long it takes for a case to reach court? Months! Years."

"Remember," replied George, "it's different here. Hopefully it won't take as long because this is the 1850s. It has to be different."

"At least one of us is being positive. I guess we just wait and see what happens."

George was right. It was only three weeks before the boys had their day in court, yet the wait seemed endless. On their first day in prison, they were separated into their own cells due to the severity of the crime with which they were accused. The lockup housed ten cells in total. Most of the cells were full of children. These were the children who spent their days walking the streets stealing wallets and purses from unsuspecting adults. Every day children appeared in court charged with theft. Some of them were referred to as 'lads-men', that is, children who stole for criminal bosses while 'mudlarks' were those children who stole from barges on rivers. The big cities such as London and Bristol saw a rise in criminal activity during the nineteenth century as so many families were very poor. Food was scarce and, sadly, crime was the way in which many families survived.

In the cells, the beds were hard and the blanket was rough and prickly. The stone floor was cold and the food mainly consisted of porridge, bread and water. The jailer was kind enough to lend the boys some books from his childrens' library to pass the time, mostly Charles Dickens, as there weren't many children's authors in the nineteenth century. The boys were grateful to have something to pass the time which was far better than sitting on a bed all day, waiting. Once a day they were let out of their cells for fifteen minutes to sit at the window for some fresh air on the opposite side of the room.

Early one morning, the boys were woken by a constable who informed them they would be appearing in court. The boys wearily rose from their beds, slipped on their shoes and waited for their cell door to open. They were ushered into a waiting cart where they were taken to the Bristol Guildhall.

The boys stood in the dock as the judge entered the room and sat down at his big mahogany desk. He peered over his glasses and looked at the boys with a stern face. The court clerk read out the charge of murder brought against William and George. "Well," said the judge, "this is a very serious charge indeed." A policeman who had been assigned to the case stated the facts to the court – that a worker had seen the boys running from Mr Babbage's room, after which the worker went directly to his room to find him dead. The policeman went onto say that the boys were seen at Bristol station where they did their best to evade police. The judge asked the boys whether they were innocent or guilty.

"Innocent," they answered.

"Then why does an innocent man run?" he asked.

"Well, sir," replied William, "when we entered Mr Babbage's room he was already dead so we panicked and ran."

"We are innocent," cried George. "You must believe us."

"I will believe the facts of the case. That is my job," replied the judge. "And the facts of the case are that you had Mr Babbage's blood on your coat when you were caught."

"I leant over him to see his face. I thought he was sleeping."

"And what business did you have to enter his room to begin with?"

What could William say? That Mr Babbage killed his father who was from the future? William couldn't think of anything remotely plausible to say.

"Well then," said the judge, "an innocent man would have been able to answer that question and a guilty man, or young boy, as in the case of yourselves, would not."

The jury of twelve men left the room shortly afterwards to deliberate. William and George were led out of the dock into a narrow corridor outside the courtroom and waited nervously. An hour later, the boys were led back into the court and stood at the dock, waiting for the judge who soon reappeared. Facing the jury, the Judge asked whether they had reached a decision.

"We have, Your Honour," responded an older gentleman.

"And what, say, is your decision?"

The feeling William and George had, standing in the dock, knowing that the rest of their life would be determined by those twelve men was terrifying. George could barely stand. He was so nervous he felt his legs might buckle right underneath him. The verdict was read out. One simple word that could change the lives of William and George forever.

One word that would determine freedom or imprisonment. William couldn't bear the suspense.

"Guilty!"

The boys couldn't believe what they just heard. It was as though the world had just stopped. "What?" gasped William. "What?"

George's legs did in fact give way and he collapsed onto the floor. William was so dumbfounded he didn't even register that his best friend was no longer standing right next to him. A policeman went to George's aid and helped him up onto his feet again. Unsteady, George stood shaking in front of the judge.

"We are innocent! Please, sir, we are innocent," shouted William.

The judge picked up his gavel and banged it on the table. "Order in the courtroom," he bellowed. "The court has decided. Under normal circumstances I would sentence you to death by hanging, however, on account of your youth I therefore sentence you to spend the rest of your natural lives doing hard labour, confined to the isle of Australia. This sentence will be carried out immediately.

"Australia!" whimpered George.

"No!" shouted William.

Again, the judge picked up his gavel, raised it high above his head and brought it down with an almighty thud on the wooden desk. The deafening sound vibrated around the courtroom. "Case closed."

"Wait!" shouted a voice from the back of the room. "Please wait!" Everyone in the courtroom turned around to see a woman standing at the door. William and George spun around and recognised the person standing there. It was Mrs Maguire. She looked unkempt and out of breath, as though she had been running. Strands of hair hung down the sides of her face and her usually neat bun on top of her head was falling out. "There's been a mistake," she yelled, approaching the bench.

"Who—"

Before the judge could finish asking who she was, she told him that the boys were under her care at the workhouse and that they could not have killed Mr Babbage.

"And why not?" asked the judge.

"Because it was me!"

Every person in the courtroom gasped in total shock. Astonished, the judge ordered everyone to be quiet and asked her to proceed.

Mrs Maguire explained that she went to see Mr Babbage, her uncle, to retrieve some property he had seized that belonged to her. He told her he would not give it back and produced a gun, and aimed it at her. He fired the gun but it didn't go off. He fired it a second time and again, nothing happened. Mr Babbage was enraged at this point, trying to get the gun working. In the melee he turned the gun around to find out what was wrong with it and it went off when he accidentally pulled the trigger. He shot himself, fell onto his bed and died.

Being a fair man, the judge halted sentencing of the boys until Mrs Maguire's version of events could be confirmed by a second coroner. The boys therefore remained in custody and several days later, the coroner returned to the court with new evidence. He had found a set of notes that wasn't submitted to the court. It stated that small particles of gunpowder was found on Mr Babbage's right hand. This new evidence confirmed that Mr Babbage had indeed pulled the trigger. William and George were duly set free and walked out of the courtroom with Mrs Maguire. She had saved their lives. Standing on the steps of the courthouse, George threw his arms around Mrs Maguire. "We can't thank you enough."

"He's right," said William. "We are so grateful to you. How did you know about our case?"

"After my altercation with Mr Babbage, I fled and returned to Surrey. A couple of weeks later I read about two young men called William Pritchard and George Fraser in the newspaper. I had to come and help, especially as I knew you were innocent."

"When are you returning to Surrey?" asked George.

"Not until later today. Five o'clock is my train. What will you do now?" she asked.

"I'm pretty hungry for some proper food," said William, laughing.

"Come on then," replied Mrs Maguire.

They found a nearby tea shop and sat down for lunch. William told Mrs Maguire everything, that his father had died and that Mr Babbage killed him, which was why they had come back. Mrs Maguire felt very sad for William as she had lost her own parents when she was very young. "Simply an awful situation," she told the boys. They sat in the cafe for most of the afternoon. The boys ate as if their lives depended on it. For the past few weeks their diet consisted of mainly bread and water so they were happy to eat cucumber sandwiches, cakes and scones with jam and cream. Mrs Maguire said that Tommy, Maisie and Albert were all doing very well, although Tommy fell out of a tree and spent two days in hospital with a mild concussion.

"Hospital!" said George. "That's it!"

"What is?" asked William.

"The hospital might have a record of your dad. If he was buried, then he might have been to a hospital first."

"Well done, George," said William excitedly. "It's probably a long shot but definitely worth a try." William gulped the remainder of his drink and stood up. "Mrs Maguire, we need to get back to London."

"And I need to get back to Surry," she replied. Mrs Maguire paid the bill and they walked to Bristol train station together.

Before boarding her train, Mrs Maguire pulled out of her purse a stamp and an envelope with her address in Surry. The stamp was a penny black, which had a picture of a young Queen Victoria. "Please write to us," she begged. William promised he would and placed the stamp and envelope in his pocket. Mrs Maguire boarded her train while William and George waited for the next train to London.

Sitting on the platform, William apologised to George. "I'm sorry that I got you into this mess, you know, prison."

"I would have come with you anyway."

CHAPTER 25

In the absence of modern-day transport, it was a long walk from Paddington station to St Brigid's hospital but they finally arrived, tired and weary. William had a few schillings his mother had given him for his journey. It was money that she kept from the times she travelled through the trees as a teenager. She never knew when she would need it and this was most definitely the time.

Unlike the library, the hospital was unfamiliar to William. It was a big old brick building with rows of windows on either side. Inside, a large entrance hall was crowded with sick people waiting to be seen. Not knowing where to begin, the boys saw a nurse walking into a corridor, looked at each other and began to follow her. She passed a small room of lockers where white coats hung on a nearby rack. A few minutes later, the boys left the room wearing the white coats and stethoscopes around their necks. "Best if I do all the talking," whispered William as they approached a big desk in the foyer.

A young woman wearing her hair up under a frilly white cap looked up. "Can I 'elp you, Doctor?" she asked in a cockney accent.

"Ah yes... We're looking for the records office," said William in a deep voice. "In particular, names of patients who have passed away in the last six months."

The nurse looked confused. "Don't keep no records 'ere, sir. The 'ospital is too busy to keep in mind the comings and goings of the sick. We just treat 'em and they leave. Most of 'em die 'ere. As for me, I don't even venture into the wards. All them sick people with their diseases, why I'm just as sure to get sick and die just looking at 'em, I am."

"Er, right then," replied William. "What if someone was treated here and they had been killed by a gunshot. Is that an incident you might remember?"

The nurse sat back in her chair thinking. "Hmm, don't s'pose I would. It ain't nothin' new gettin' struck by a bullet nowadays. London ain't safe no more."

Realising this was a dead end, William looked at George and rolled his eyes. "Let's go." They began walking away.

"Mind you," the nurse went on, "I do remember a man with a bullet wound who only 'ad one hand. Strange fella."

"What?" William and George spun around and returned to the desk. "What did you say?" asked William. "What happened to him?"

"Well, I say it's strange as he 'ad all these little bottles of medicine on him. Just walked in off the street, he did."

"What happened to him?" repeated William. "This is very important."

"Oh, he got fixed up a'right. I do remember that. Can't remember much after that, I'm afraid to say."

"Did you find out his name?" asked George.

"Well now. Lemme see. Peter… No…"

"David," said William. "Was it David?"

"Yes! That's it. David. Said he was a doctor an' all. Also said he got shot in a park by robbers. Like I said, London ain't safe no more."

"He's alive then?" asked William.

"Assume so. Walked out that front door a week later, he did. Lucky one, that one. Most of 'em die."

"Did he say where he was going?"

"Sorry, Doctor. Can't help yer there." The nurse stood up. "Now, if you don't need nothin' else, I've finished me shift for tonight." The nurse picked up her bag, pulled on a coat and left William and George standing at the front desk.

"I can't believe it! He's alive!" William threw his arms around George and the boys hugged each other.

"William, I'm sorry," replied George. "I was sure he was dead. I checked his pulse and there wasn't a heartbeat."

"It's okay, really, it is. That whole night was crazy so I understand how you might have thought he had died."

George interjected, "And Isabel. She was all hunched over him crying her eyes out. I just wanted to get her home, I thought Babbage might come back and hurt us both."

"George, its fine, really it is. He's alive and that's all that matters. We need to concentrate on finding him now. I have an idea. Dad won't have any money so we should start with the homeless. We ask everyone we come across if they know of a man with one hand."

"Surely there can't be many men roaming the streets with one hand."

"Exactly," agreed William. "I think it's a long shot but it's a start."

It was now well after midnight. The boys decided they would find an inn for the night and begin their search in the morning. Waking early, they ate breakfast and began their search for David. They spent all day walking the streets asking just about everyone they passed whether they had seen a one-handed man. Not one person said yes and William realised it was naive of him to think that they could possibly find him in a city amongst a million people. They walked through the poor areas where overcrowded slums housed dozens of families. Young children clung to their mothers legs while they stood outside their houses in their ragged clothes, hanging washing on makeshift lines. Old people with their wrinkled faces and sunken eyes sat on the steps outside crumbling tenements. It was a dreadful sight and William felt heartbroken that he was unable to help these poorer areas. After a few days, William's money was quickly dwindling and he knew he had to return home or face living on the streets, not unlike in the poverty he had just witnessed.

Heartbroken, William realised it was time to return home. After what they had seen in the slums they couldn't stay and live on the streets. It would prove too dangerous and there was no guarantee they would ever find William's father. Begrudgingly, they set off for Bishops Park early the next morning after they spent the last of their money at the inn. Horse-drawn carriages filled the busy streets and the boys jumped onto a small bench at the back of a carriage, a space just big enough for two footmen. They hitched a ride across London, walking the last mile to Bishops Park.

"Well, here it is," said George as they arrived at the iron gates that were so familiar to them.

Reluctantly, William entered the park while George followed. "I guess it's time to go home," he said.

"William, I'm sorry we couldn't find your dad."

"So am I. Feels like I've let everyone down."

"You haven't let anyone down. The fact that you came back and risked your life to find him just shows how courageous you are. Your dad would be really proud and wherever he is, I'm sure he knows you tried your best."

"Thanks. I guess that counts for something. Come on, let's find the oak tree. It's time to go."

As the boys walked through the park, they passed the caretaker's house. The outside light shone onto the porch and they continued through the park until they noticed something very strange. George noticed it first and grabbed William's arm. The oak tree, with its thick brown trunk extending high into the sky; its branches covered with an abundance of prickly green leaves, was gone. In its place was simply a patch of grass. It was as though the tree had never existed. William fell to his knees while George just stood there, dumbfounded. Trying to open his mouth, William was speechless. He couldn't even purse his lips together to form a word.

"The... T... T... Ree..." George stammered.

"The tree," William whispered.

"Why? How?" asked George.

"What happened to it? Are we in the right park? The right year?"

"How do we get back?" asked George as the panic began to set it.

"We need the same tree, George, and now it's gone. We can't get back."

William and George sat on the grassy patch trying to figure out what to do. They had nowhere to go. William pulled his coat pockets inside out and scattered its contents onto the grass. All he had of any significance was the folded envelope and stamp that Mrs Maguire gave him to write to the children. Opening up the envelope William noticed that Mrs Maguire had written her address in Surrey on the front of the envelope. Well, he thought, he could go and see her but he didn't have the money to get there so that was futile. In any case, what would he do once he arrived? She already had three young children in her care and most likely couldn't afford to feed another two. No, that wouldn't work. He had to find a way to get home.

Just as they had run out of every idea they could possibly think of, George suggested they knock on the door of the caretaker's house and find out what had happened to the tree. At least if they had some answers they might be able to work out a way to get home. So that's exactly what they did. William gently knocked on the door. When nobody answered he knocked again. He had a strange feeling of history repeating itself, just as when he and Isabel last knocked on the door and found the notebooks in the bedroom upstairs.

"No," he said, backing away. "We can't go in. Even if someone's home. I've been here before, with Isabel, and this house and the people inside are bad."

"Alright then," whispered George. "What do we do?"

"Follow me," replied William. "Let's see what's round the back."

The boys tiptoed to the end of the porch and wandered around the back of the house where a tall fence sectioned off the park from the private garden. The grass was neatly cut and flowerbeds lined a narrow stone path that led to a timber shed at the bottom of the garden.

"Over there," said George pointing to the shed. "I wonder what's in there."

"Let's find out."

Feeling apprehensive, the boys decided not to open the shed door but instead peer through a small window around the side. Inside the far corner of the shed was a figure. It was a little hard to see through the dirty window, but it moved, it swayed from side to side. When William pulled his sleeve down and wiped it across the window it became clear that the figure was actually the shape of a person. Dressed in a long black cape, the person swayed, slowly lifting their arms into the air and swaying from side to side as if they were in a trance. The boys couldn't see who it was until the figure turned around rather suddenly and glanced at the window. William jumped with fright when he realised it was a woman whom he recognised. She glared straight at him, her eyes squinted as the two locked eyes for a split second, yet, for William, it felt like a whole minute.

William ran first, then George. They ran as fast as they could away from the shed, out of the garden and away from the house. They ran out of the park and stopped outside the entrance. Bending down with his hands on his knees, William stood there, catching his breath.

"What just happened?" asked George. "Did you see the lady in the shed? I couldn't see much but she looked like some sort of witch or something. Did you see?"

"Yes, I saw her," William said, puffing. "Didn't you see her face? Didn't you recognise her?"

"No. Should I?" asked George.

"Yes! That was my mother."

"What?" replied George. "How is that possible?"

"I don't understand. What is she doing in 1851? And how did she get here?"

"Maybe," said George, in between breaths, "maybe she had something to do with the removal of the oak tree. What do you think?"

"Could be but why would she remove the tree when she knows we need it to get home? Why would she do that to us, George?" asked William, tears welling up in his eyes.

"It's just a thought. Maybe she's here to help us get back home. For all we know, she could be doing some sort of magic to bring it back."

"Well then," said William. "Do we go back to the shed and find out what's going on?"

"I think it's the only way," answered George. "After all, she's your mum and she loves you. She wouldn't hurt you. You know that."

The boys agreed to head back into the park and confront William's mother. When they returned to the shed she was gone. Upon entering the shed, the only remnants that remained was a big chalk circle on the floor where she stood. The smell of burning incense lingered in the air. William walked around the small shed looking for anything that his mother might have left behind. The shed was fairly empty except for several shelves that ran along one side of the wall. The top shelf was littered with various gardening tools, a small hoe, a long wire rake and a shovel with the end covered in dirt. The two bottom shelves were empty. "Nothing here," said William as he picked up objects and placed them back down.

"Same," reported George from the other side of the shed.

"Well then," said William, "we'll wait right here in this shed. She might come back and if she doesn't at least we have a place to sleep for the night."

The boys sat in the shed and waited. When darkness fell, the chilly night air crept through the shed so the boys wrapped themselves up in their warm jackets and fell asleep. George was first to wake early the next morning and noticed that the shed door was open. It seemed odd because he was sure it was closed when they fell asleep. As he slowly sat up, he noticed muddy footprints that had circled the very spot where he and William slept. Nudging William, he said, "Quick, wake up. Someone's been here."

William sat up and saw the footsteps circle back towards the door. "They're big footprints so it can't be Mum," replied William.

"That's what I thought," said George. "Maybe they belong to the person living in the house."

The boys quickly got up and walked towards the open door. "Look out here," said William. "The footsteps head back towards the park."

"Someone's been in here while we slept," said George. "That's really creepy."

"It's weird that they didn't wake us. Can't have been the occupants in the house or they would have kicked us out. That said, I think we've outdone our welcome."

George clutched his stomach. "I'm starving. Let's head back into town and get some food. We might be lucky and find a soup kitchen."

"In the 1800s? I doubt it but it's worth a try."

The boys crept out of the shed and found a narrow space at the rear of the shed, jumped over the fence, straight into the park and onto the dewy grass. They didn't dare walk past the house for fear of being seen. As they headed towards the park gate, it soon became clear that someone was following them. The footsteps got louder with each step. William didn't dare look behind. He hoped the footsteps would fade away but they didn't. When they got louder he stopped and spun around. Standing right in front of him was his father. William and George stood there in a complete state of shock.

"William," whispered David.

"Dad? Is it really you?" William couldn't believe his father was standing right in front of him.

"But you died," said George. "I saw it with my own eyes. I swear, William, he was dead..."

"It's all right," interrupted David. "Got a hug for your old man?"

"You bet!" William wrapped his arms around his father once again and it felt wonderful. "What on earth happened, Dad?"

"Okay, boys, I'll explain everything. George, you were right in assuming I was dead but the bullet wound wasn't fatal. When you found me I was in a state of shock, medically known as hypovolemic shock. This causes very low blood pressure so if you checked for a pulse, it's very likely that you may not have found one as my heart was barely beating. When I woke some time later on the grass, I found some bottles of medicine and I knew that one of my children had been back through the trees as these types of medicine weren't available in the mid-1800s. So I opened the morphine and gave myself a shot to dull the pain which allowed me to administer the antibiotics. When I tried to get up a young man came to help me and we managed to get to the hospital."

"What happened then?" asked William.

"The young man thought that if he were seen with me arriving at the hospital, the doctors might assume he was responsible so he left me at the entrance."

"That's awful," said George.

"No, George, he was a good man to have helped me."

David put his arm around George's shoulder. "George, you saved my life because you left the medicine on the ground. I certainly would have died if you hadn't done that. And, William, what a brave man you were to risk so much by travelling back to get the medicine. I'm in awe that you had the sense to do that as well as finding the right medicine. I've never felt so proud of you. In my absence your mother's done a wonderful job raising you."

"Oh my gosh! Mum!"

"What is it, son?"

"We saw her. In the shed behind Mr Brown's house in the park. She's a witch!"

"What do you mean?"

"Well," replied William. "She was chanting something really odd, she had a black cape on, she was standing in a big circle and when she turned around I saw her face."

"It was definitely her," interrupted George. "As soon as she saw us, we ran."

"No," replied David. "It wasn't Mum."

"I know it was her," said an agitated William. "I swear. When she saw us, she was just as shocked as we were."

"William, I need to tell you something. The woman you saw is Raven."

"I'm confused," said George.

"Yes, Dad, *please* explain."

"Your mother is a twin. Raven is actually your aunt. You see, William, your mother was born on 7th September..."

"Yes, Dad, I know Mum's birthday..."

"In 1533."

A gobsmacked William couldn't believe what he just heard. "Do you mean to tell me that Mum is over four hundred years old?"

"Yes, son. She was born in a village just outside London on the very same day as Queen Elizabeth I. The baby girls were separated at birth because her mother was very poor and couldn't raise both girls. She already had a son and was too poor to feed three children. She couldn't choose which child to keep so the Church decided that the firstborn would stay with their mother. The girls grew up with different families, yet they were, I guess you could call it, witches.

"Wow," said William. "Now it's all starting to make sense. So my mother is a witch and is five hundred years old?"

"It's incredible," said George. "How did your mum end up in the twenty-first century then?"

"She and Raven found out that they were sisters and didn't got along. Raven was very jealous of your mother because their mother never got over losing your mum. Raven wanted to seek revenge and in order for your mother to escape, the only way she knew how was to travel through the trees and create a new life for herself. Then she met me…"

"And the rest is history," said William.

"That's right," replied David.

"Oh, Dad. We can't get back home. When we came back to find what happened to you after Babbage shot you, we returned to the park to go home and the tree was gone!"

"It's true," uttered George. "It's like it never existed. And now we can't get home. What do we do?"

Looking at the boys, David sensed their anguish for he felt the same way too. "Yes. I know the tree is gone. I've been coming here every day since leaving the hospital in the hope that you would come back and find me. When I returned yesterday, I also noticed that it had just disappeared."

"But trees don't just disappear," said George.

"Exactly," replied David. "The fact that Raven has shown herself here in 1851 and the oak tree simply disappearing into thin air indicates to me that she's responsible. I just can't figure out why."

The three men who stood together in the park were all thinking the same thing. They had to find Raven.

CHAPTER 26

When David's gunshot wound had healed he was released from hospital and wandered the streets for several days. A few kind market sellers gave him a little food to eat and at night he slept in a narrow alleyway at the rear of a button factory. One particular morning, he was woken by a man who introduced himself. His name was John Carr and he was a missionary. Mr Carr told David he had seen him in the hospital and prayed for him as he didn't think he would survive his first night. He was delighted to see that David was indeed alive and after seeing his living conditions, he wanted to help him find more suitable accommodation. So they set off that morning to St. Martin-in-the-Fields church, next to Trafalgar Square, where David was introduced to a priest.

Upon finding out that David was a doctor and only having one useful hand, it was clear that he was unable to find work in a hospital. However, the priest thought he could be useful in helping the poor. David jumped at the chance so it was agreed that David would use his medical knowledge in exchange for accommodation and meals at the rectory. David had finally found his calling. He now had a purpose. Word quickly spread that a local doctor was helping the poorer people of London. People from all over the city came to David to help cure all sorts of conditions, from minor ailments to more serious concerns like tuberculosis and typhoid. Men who had engaged in bar fights turned up, bloodied and bruised, nursing their wounds. For anything that required more technical handiwork, Mr Carr proved to be a very useful assistant. It was a lovely partnership. David now had a comfortable place in which to live and was able to practice his beloved medicine and Mr Carr, upon finishing his mission in Africa, was able to continue helping the local community. The two men became very good friends and eyebrows weren't even raised when, early one morning, David returned from his morning stroll with William and George accompanying him. It was assumed that the two boys were ill and David kept up the pretense by bandaging George's head and tying a sling around William's shoulder.

After sharing a breakfast of porridge with warm milk and a pot of tea, the trio set off to find Raven. Bishops Park would be their first stop. They boarded an omnibus from Trafalgar Square and huddled together inside the dark and musty carriage. With two rows of eleven seats facing each other, William and George sat opposite David. The carriage was full and there was no ventilation except when the door opened to let people on and off. The straw covered floor, which was primarily used was to keep people's feet warm, was wet and muddy by the time they reached the other side of London. Ladies' crinolines that hung to the floor soaked up much of the mud, while their parasols often jabbed into someone's shoe when they stood up to disembark. Eventually the trio made it back to Bishops Park and headed straight for the shed at the back of the caretaker's house.

"This way," said William as he and George walked via the back fence that led directly into the caretaker's garden. "Nobody from the house will see us if we jump the fence." So they jumped the fence and carefully walked around the side of the shed. Peering into the window, the shed looked empty.

"She's not here," whispered George.

"We'll go inside and look around anyway. Come on," replied David.

David, closely followed by William then George, walked around the front of the shed. David slowly turned the knob and opened the door. As it creaked, he stepped ever so quietly into the shed. Seeing that it was empty, he let out a sigh of relief and entered. "Come on," he said. "It's empty."

The boys stepped into the empty space and looked around. "Well, she's definitely not here," said William. "To be honest, I feel relieved. I don't know why but the whole thought of meeting Raven just scares the wits out of me."

All of a sudden, a gust of wind rose up and ripped through the shed blowing leaves and debris all the way up to the ceiling. A loud bang sounded as the door slammed shut. David and the boys quickly turned around and, to their astonishment, there stood the witch called Raven. The wind whipped her long black hair up over her face. Her long black dress covered her pasty white skin. She stood there glaring at David, then laid her eyes upon William.

"R-R-Raven!" stammered David. "Is it really you?"

The woman in front of them just stood and stared for a moment. Her wicked eyes wide with anger.

"We mean you no harm," interjected William. "Er... We... Just want to get back home through the oak tree..."

David placed his hand on William's shoulder, an indication that he would do the talking. "That's right. The tree is gone and because you are here, we need to know if it was you who removed it." David waited for a response. He felt threatened, scared.

The witch took a step forward. William and George took two steps backwards. She was standing right in front of David, who hadn't moved at all. He wanted to show her that he was not scared. Looking him up and down, she spoke in an unusually soft voice. "So... You are the husband of that dear sister of mine? Does that mean we are sister and brother-in-law?"

"Well, er, yes. I suppose we are."

"Well then," Raven continued, walking towards the boys, "what have we here?"

William began to sweat. His heart was pounding and his hands felt clammy. He thought if she was powerful enough to remove the existence of a five-hundred-year-old oak tree then she was capable of anything.

"Hello, nephew," she whispered into William's ear.

"Did you remove the oak tree?" William asked.

"Well, I might have," she said laughing.

David grabbed William's arm and pulled him away from Raven. "Stay away from my son," he said sternly.

Raven stepped back and locked eyes on David. "I'm quite special," she said. "You see, I can conjure up spells. Any spell you like. I can make people sick, make people die, make trees magic... I can even make trees disappear!"

"It *was* you!" interrupted William. "We knew you did it. But why?"

"Maybe you should ask George," she replied, smirking.

"What is going on, George?" demanded David.

"I'll tell you what's going on," replied George. "Give us the amulet and we'll return the tree so you can go home."

"What amulet?" asked William. "What are you talking about?"

"Oh, come on," replied George. "You *must* know what I mean."

Raven interrupted. "The one that was given to your mother five hundred years ago. Our mother gave it to her when she was taken away as a baby and I need it. It should have been given to *me*!"

"Us!" said George. "It belongs to us."

William looked at George, puzzled. "What do you mean by *us*, George? What are you talking about?"

Raven laughed again. "Haven't you worked it out? Why, George is my son!"

Both William and David gasped in shock. William could barely comprehend what he had just heard. "Is it true?" he asked George. "Is it really true?"

"Yes, it's true," replied George.

"The amulet is very powerful," said Raven. "It must be in my possession in order for me to cast the spell that will make me immortal. I realised the only way to get it was to send George through the trees to infiltrate your family and retrieve it. I cast a set of spells on some of the trees in the park so I could find my sister. By befriending you, he would have access to your house and find the amulet without arousing suspicion. You see, as beautiful as I am, I do not wish to grow old. I do not wish to spend my life watching the wrinkles appear on my face through the passage of time. I do not want to see my long, thick ,silky hair turn grey. I want to live forever and there can be no higher power in life than to be immortal."

"So," continued William, looking straight at George. "All this time you weren't really my friend?"

"YES!" replied George. "It was all a big lie. The day you found my coin of Queen Elizabeth II in the workhouse was no accident. I deliberately let you find it to befriend you, so we could travel back to your home. Then I could get into your house and I did, but I couldn't find the amulet anywhere."

"Did you actually live in the workhouse for three years or was that a lie too?"

George rolled his eyes as if William was stupid. "Of course not, I was there for a week, silly. Remember that my mother is a witch so she changed time to make it appear that I had been there three years."

"But how did you know we were going to be at that particular workhouse?"

"Oh, you poor, silly boy," interjected Raven. "Simon Brown made sure of that. I made a deal with him that he'd be rich when the amulet was returned to me and, of course, he obliged. He's easily led, you know."

"Yes, we know," said William. "He's also been selling children to the workhouses."

Raven chuckled then began laughing. Her laugh got louder and louder until the window in the shed shattered. Hundreds of shards of glass fell onto the floor.

"So where is it, then?" asked George. "Give it to us and we'll put tree back so you can all go home."

"But we don't have it. Honestly," said William. "I've never seen it in my life. If my mother had something so precious, I'm sure I'd know about it and I don't, so that's why I'm telling you we don't have it."

"Yes, we do," said David. He held out his hand and there in the palm of his hand was the amulet. The small round coin with three small stones of aquamarine, citrine and peridot at each point made up a larger triangle of one solid diamond. "Return the tree then you can have it," he said.

"Oh, my amulet! My beautiful, precious amulet." Raven threw herself at David.

"Not so fast," he bellowed, closing his fist and clenching the amulet tightly.

Raven's face grew angry. Her eyes squinted and she pursed her lips with a mean looking scowl. "Give it to me," she roared. "Or I will cast a spell on your precious, beloved son. I'll make every bone in his body turn to rubber so if you think life is hard with one hand imagine how hard his life would be with no bones."

"Alright! Alright!" said David, his voice trembling. "Here it is. Just leave William alone and put the tree back. We'll leave right now and you'll never have to see us again." David placed the amulet on the floor and backed away. He clutched William as he moved closer to the door. Raven threw herself on the floor, her black hair blowing wildly then settling back down over her bony shoulders. She scooped up the amulet with both hands and held it tightly against her chest. "The tree," said David. "You have what you wanted now return the tree and let my son go home."

"Home?" shouted Raven. "And where is *your* home, David? You're in a mess, aren't you? Being stuck here in 1851. Do you miss your wife and daughter?"

"That's enough!" shouted George. The room fell silent and a completely shocked Raven spun around towards her son.

"What did you say?" she bellowed.

"Mother, you have what you wanted. Now put the tree back."

"Don't think so," said Raven, laughing.

"We agreed that nobody would get hurt, that William and Isabel would be okay. You promised."

"Oh, now isn't that sweet. My son standing up for them. Whose side are you on? Mine or theirs?" Raven produced a small bottle of liquid from her pocket and dangled it in front of George. "You know, George, this little bottle of magic will return the tree but I'm not feeling the love from you so I think... I think... think..." she repeated as she paced back and forth. "I think I'll leave you all here."

"No!" cried George. "Mother, take me with you."

With the bottle of liquid still in her hand, Raven shouted, "Goodbye!" She headed for the door. David had to act fast and ran towards Raven. He grabbed hold of her arm and pulled her back into the shed. "Let go of me!" she demanded.

"Put the tree back!"

A scuffle ensued. William, seeing his father struggling to grab the bottle out of Raven's hand, ran to help him. Raven clutched the bottle so tightly, her hand was turning blue. She was determined not to give it up. "Let me go!" she demanded. "You're hurting me! Help me, George!"

George scurried over and pushed William and David out of the way. "Here, give it to me," he told her, holding out his hand. Raven let go of the bottle, dropping it into George's hand. She stood up, out of breath from the scuffle.

"There's a good boy," she said, beaming.

William and David couldn't believe the betrayal. It was as if their whole lives had just slipped away, now that George was in possession of the bottle. Then, all of a sudden, George turned to William and held out his hand. "This is for you," he said.

"Oh, George," cried William.

"Take it."

William took the bottle and handed it to David.

"What did you do?" demanded Raven. "What did you do?"

"I'm sorry, Mother" said George. He loved his mother yet, for the first time ever, he now saw her for the evil person she really was. He realised that his own mother had put him in a very dangerous position by sending him through the trees to obtain the amulet. He also realised that her need for power and immortality was more important than her love for him. He felt angry, hurt and let down. He suddenly realised that true love came from his friends, William and Isabel, and he couldn't believe that he didn't see it until now.

Brushing her hair away from her face, Raven sniggered. "Have your stupid potion, I *still* have the amulet. I don't need you, George, I don't need any of you because I am now the most powerful witch in the world and I can do ANYTHING!" Raven began walking out of the shed. She stopped and looked back at her enemies. "Live in fear, boys, for I *will* return." She strolled down the path towards the caretaker house. George ran after her.

"Mother!" he shouted. "Give the amulet back. It doesn't belong to you."

Raven became enraged. She stopped when George stood right in front of her, blocking her way. David and William also stood next to George in defiance. George grabbed his mother, pulled her towards him and hugged her. He held her so tightly that she couldn't move. "I love you," he whispered.

Raven pulled away from her son and produced a small gold leaf from her sleeve. She chanted:

> "This gold leaf that I do bear
> turn to dust and in despair
> his skin will blister and then burn
> to live a life he will yearn."

The leaf turned into dust in the palm of Raven's hand. She held her hand up to her mouth and blew the dust in George's face. George screamed in agony and fell to the ground, cupping his face with his hands. William pulled off his shirt and began gently wiping the dust away from George's face which began blistering with red hot welts. "I'm sorry, William," whimpered George as he lay dying on the ground.

"You don't have to apologise," replied William. "I know you didn't mean it. You were forced to. She was your mother and you trusted her."

"I'm a bad person."

"No, George. You weren't to know that she was never going to replace the tree. You didn't know. You're just a kid, like me."

"You're a true friend, Will. You always were. I just didn't realise it."

"You didn't know what friendship was. Neither did I until I met you." William placed George's head on his lap and gently stroked his hair, trying to make his last moments as comfortable as possible. "What an adventure we've had," cried William as the tears rolled down his cheeks.

"Yes." George closed his eyes. "Time… To… Go… Brother." George slowly placed a small pouch into the palm of William's hand and was gone. Killed by the hand of his evil, wicked mother, who was also gone.

"Oh, George," cried William. He was so heartbroken that he didn't even acknowledge the pouch in his hand.

David bent down next to William and gently rubbed his back. "I'm sorry, son. Let's give him a proper burial."

William placed the pouch in his pocket and helped David carry George's body back into the shed. They laid him down gently and agreed to bury him under the elm tree where George first travelled. It felt like the right place for George's final resting place. They prayed for George and after his burial they made their way back to the grassy area where the oak tree used to stand.

"What do we do now, Dad?" asked William.

"I just don't know, son."

William sat on the grass and felt a little jab. Reaching into his pocket, he pulled out the little brown pouch that George had given him. It had a soft leathery texture, stitching around the top and a drawstring to open it. William pulled the string open and pulled out a small piece of paper with an inscription . Upon reading the words, William began to shake. His heart began pounding.

> "A tree, this one they call the oak
> nay gone, this spell shall revoke
> three drops of aurora blue on site
> shall return the tree before to-night"

"Dad!" William yelled.

"What's wrong?"

"It's the spell to replace the tree! Look!"

William handed David the bottle and read the inscription over and over again. Looking at William, David was speechless.

"He did it!" William hollered. "George did it! He must have known we needed the potion and the spell...."

"And when he hugged her, he slipped it from her pocket."

"Then he gave it to me. Oh, George, you did it!"

"So how does it work?" asked David excitedly.

"I don't know but I guess we sprinkle the liquid right here where the tree should stand and say the magic words."

"Are you quite sure about that?" asked David. "We don't have a second chance."

"It's in the spell. Three drops at the exact spot where the tree was and..."

"It's returned before nightfall" interrupted David.

Without hesitation, William tipped the bottle slowly until three drops of blue liquid fell onto the ground as he chanted the spell. David and William stood back and waited. All of a sudden, the earth beneath their feet began to shake. A small root pierced the ground and up it came, passing William and David's heads. As the root got higher, it became bigger until it formed a thick, round trunk. Branches began spurting from the trunk, whipping through the air as the tree grew taller and taller. And then it stopped. Standing right in front of William was the big oak tree, in all of its glory, just the way it had always looked.

"Woo hoo!" shouted William.

"Wonderful!" shouted David back as the two jumped up and down, ran around the tree and hugged each other.

"Thank you, George," said William. "This is the best gift you could ever give me."

"William," said David solemnly. "It's time to go."

"I know."

"I can't go back because of my hand, but it's okay because I've made a life for myself here helping people. I can still use my medical knowledge and that's a great comfort to me."

"I can stay with you, Dad."

"No, you can't, son. With every inch of my being I wish you could but we both know it's just not possible. You have a wonderful life waiting for you, a life with Isabel and Mum. They need you, you're the man of the house now."

"Dad, we've said our goodbyes before and I don't think I can do it again. It'll kill me."

David hugged his son tightly. "You'll be okay. Just remember that I'm alive and knowing that you and Isabel are looking after each other gives me all the happiness and strength I need."

"I promise to look after the girls, Dad. I promise."

"You hold all the power, William. You can time travel. Imagine all the possibilities. You can change the world for the better. I love you so much, William, and I'm so proud of you. Now go before I start crying. Again!"

"I love you too, Dad. I'll come back to see you. I promise."

William reluctantly placed his hands on the tree and, just like magic had intended, he was gone.

PART 2 - 1533

PART TWO

CHAPTER 27

On 7 September, in the year 1533, hundreds of babies were born in England, which was nothing unusual. However, one of those babies was very special because she was born a princess in a palace just outside London. She was named Elizabeth and would rule England one day. Another baby girl was born in a small cottage on the palace estate and she was named Gudrun. While Elizabeth grew up as the daughter of King Henry VIII, Gudrun's parents worked as servants in the very court in which Elizabeth was raised. As the girls were the same age, they spent much of their childhood together and were very close. In the summer they climbed trees, rode horses and lay in fields of long grass, wondering who they would marry. Elizabeth received an excellent education and was proficient in six languages, including Latin. Her education was of the utmost importance as the art of public speaking would prove a very important skill in her future. Gudrun, on the other hand, went to the local school and learnt the basics of reading, writing and maths.

Over the years, however, Elizabeth and Gudrun grew apart. Elizabeth was very busy attending fancy balls and mixing with lords and ladies, while Gudrun began spending more time with her mother who became ill. It began with a rash that appeared on her skin which caused little blisters to break out over her face. People in the village were unkind and didn't want anything to do with her so she sought the help of an apothecary who administered sandalwood and geranium oil for her skin. The local villagers thought that Gudrun's mother was concocting spells, which was actually the oil for her skin, so it was assumed she was a witch.

This was most unfortunate as witchcraft in the sixteenth century was illegal and anyone who acted the slightest bit odd was accused of being a witch and was therefore killed by order of the King. The hysteria surrounding witchcraft became so ridiculous that anybody who owned a domestic cat was accused of being a witch. The King paid men to travel around England on the lookout for witches and Gudrun's mother was therefore brought to court where she was accused of witchcraft and sentenced to death. At the young age of twelve, Gudrun was left without a mother and was utterly devastated. She vowed to avenge her mother's death. The only way she could do this was to learn the art of witchcraft and cast spells on those who had wrongly accused her mother. Over the years, witchcraft came naturally to Gudrun for she was very good at concocting spells. She changed her name to Raven, sought out other witches in the county and at night they would all meet in the forest and cast spells on those who had wronged them.

Farmers had their crops die and cattle also died in mysterious circumstances.

When the King died, he was succeeded by his son, Edward VI, who was only nine years old. Edward's reign was short lived, for he died at fifteen, and in 1558, young Princess Elizabeth was crowned Queen of England and reigned for the next forty-four years. Elizabeth proved to be an excellent ruler. She was strong. She was courageous and led her country in defeating wars against other nations.

In 1562 a new law, called the Elizabethan Witchcraft Act, passed which only allowed a witch to be killed if that witch had harmed another person. One evening, in the Summer of 1563, Raven was riding her horse to the forest where she met her witch friends for their weekly meeting. As her horse galloped through the forest, her long black tresses blowing in the wind, she was set upon by Griffin and James Williams, two brothers who made their careers as highway robbers. The brothers were known to the local villagers for they spent their days making a nuisance of themselves by stealing food and at night they held up travellers and stole all of their possessions.

Seeing Raven coming their way, they saw an opportunity to rob an innocent girl who would not be able to defend herself against the two of them. They rode their horses up beside her, grabbed the reigns from her hands and yanked, slowing the horse down until it came to a stop. They pulled her off her beloved horse and stole it. "Please return my horse to me," she begged. "For I am so far away from home I cannot walk it."

Laughing, the brothers pulled out her possessions from the saddle bag. Griffin found a small leather bag that contained a few coins. He counted the coins, shoved them in his pocket and threw the bag over his shoulder.

James picked up a bigger bag that was tied to the horse's back. "Lookee 'ere," he said, pulling out several rocks of turquoise and quartz. They glistened under the light of the moon and James studied them for a moment before digging into the bag to find several small jars of different coloured liquids. "She's none but a witch!" he exclaimed and smashed the jars onto the ground. Seeing the liquid trickling from the broken glass, Raven tried desperately to scoop up her potions but it was no use. The liquid seeped through her fingers and onto to the ground, disappearing into the earth.

"Brother," said Griffin as he glared at Raven, who was now sitting on the ground, her arms and legs bloodied from being pushed off the horse. "We must go. The witch is but worthless. She does not carry any possessions that benefit us."

Raven stayed put but did not fear the men. She was already thinking about what spell she would conjure up to exact her revenge on them.

"Aye," replied James. "We go and leave the witch here for we are not killers."

The brothers mounted their horses and rode off with Raven's horse, leaving a trail of dust behind them. Raven hobbled unsteadily to her feet and began the long walk home. It took several hours until she reached a clearing where her small house stood. By the time she walked through her front door, she was shivering from the cold, her knees were aching and she was exhausted. After dressing her wounds, she stoked up the fire and poured a small glass of metheglin, an ale distilled from honey and herbs, to warm her belly. She drank the ale, slumped down on her small bed and slept for most of the day. When she woke, she ate barley bread and butter as she set about exacting her revenge. She decided that these evil men must be stopped. They must be held accountable for all of their wrongdoings so, one afternoon, when she felt well enough to leave her house, she followed the brothers to a tavern. When their bellies were full of beer and they had fallen fast asleep, Raven, who was sitting at a table in a corner on the other side of the tavern, crept up to their table. Watching them in disgust as they snored away, she stood behind the brothers, pulled out a small glass jar from the pocket of her skirt and removed the cork. She sprinkled the dark liquid over her hands and splashed a few drops over the sleeping men as she closed her eyes and muttered a spell under her breath. The brothers continued to sleep and later that day, the men left the tavern, none the wiser.

However, as the following weeks ensued, strange thing started to occur. Griffin's legs began to swell up until he could no longer fit into his boots. His feet kept on swelling and within a few months he could no longer walk. His days of stealing horses, crops, food and making a general nuisance of himself were gone. He spent the rest of his days in bed having his mother bring his meals to his bedside.

James, on the other hand, had an undisclosed heart condition. Not only did his legs swell but the blood vessels in his heart also began to swell. He began suffering from shortness of breath, then felt pins and needles in his arms, all of which was happening while his legs were swelling up. One day he was chopping firewood and, all of a sudden, he collapsed and died.

The blame was directed at Raven as the landlord of the tavern saw her cast the spell on the brothers. Some villagers felt that Raven did them all a favour and were glad that the brothers were stopped from their evildoings. They felt safe again after so many years and were willing to overlook the fact that a witch lived among them. However, it was Griffin and his mother who insisted the matter be dealt with and were not willing to let Raven get away with James's death. They were furious and decided to write a letter to Queen Elizabeth herself, requesting that the witch called Raven who lived among them be tried for murder. Queen Elizabeth was unaware that the witch in question was her childhood friend.

What piqued the Queen's interest in the case was that James and Griffin's uncle was a special advisor in her court so she agreed to the request and had her officials bring charges against Raven.

Several weeks later, in the dead of night, a group of men congregated outside Raven's house. They held torches with flames of fire that hissed and crackled as the bright orange flames lit up the sky. Raven was fast asleep in her bed when she was woken by loud banging noise on her door.

"By order of her Royal Highness, our Queen Elizabeth, open the door!" came a loud voice. Raven shot out of bed and threw a robe around herself. As she was heading towards the door, the banging continued until the door came off its hinges and fell to the floor. Standing in the middle of the room, a frightened Raven saw several men standing at the threshold.

"What is your business?" the frightened girl asked. "Whom do you seek?"

A tall man whose face mostly covered with a long black beard stepped over the door and into the small house. Looking around, he noticed the house was relatively clean. A fireplace over to the right had a big pot in which to cook. A wooden table with two chairs sat neatly in the middle of the room. Towards the back of the house was a series of shelves that had a dozen glass jars perched on them. Inside the jars were toads and frogs, spiders and several species of bugs. The man then focused his attention on the small woman standing in front of him. He pulled out a scroll of parchment, opened it and began reading. "I am the witchfinder general, appointed by our fair Queen Elizabeth. It is rumoured thou hast been practicing witchcraft. I arrest thee on suspicion of said practice."

"No!" yelled Raven. "By your good grace, I am no witch."

"It doth ye no good," said the witch-hunter as two men grabbed each of Raven's arms. She was helpless as they bundled her onto a wagon, which was more like a cage, and locked the door. Looking through a very small window at the rear of the wagon, Raven watched as the men threw their flames onto her house. The flames fireballed onto the thatched roof and roared. It only took an hour for the house to burn to the ground. By that time, Raven had been taken to a prison cell to await trial.

The prison cells were dark and damp. There was no window, no natural light, therefore it was difficult to tell if it was day or night. A small straw mattress lay on the floor in the corner of the small cell. The cold stone floor was covered in hay. Still in her nightgown, Raven lay down on the mattress, wrapped her robe around her cold body and closed her eyes. She could hear people in nearby cells talking to themselves, some shouting out for the wardens to release them. Of course nobody came. There wasn't a guard in sight so everyone in their cells were left to themselves. After several days three more women were locked up in Raven's cell. She recognised them instantly. They, too, were witches that had been caught. The three witches belonged to the same family. The elderly woman was around sixty and her two daughters, who were around thirty years of age, all huddled up together in the opposite corner of the room. They were frightened and regardless of whether or not they were innocent, they already knew their fate and that fate came soon afterwards. They were taken to court, led into the dock and found guilty of witchcraft. Raven never saw them again.

Once again, Raven was alone in her prison cell. There wasn't much to do except sleep and that is what she did. Early one morning a gaoler came to her cell and, after handing her a breakfast of stale bread and water, duly informed her that her trial date would be within the following week. He then left with his chain of keys clattering in his hand as he walked up the dark narrow staircase and disappeared. This left Raven wondering why the other witches had their trial over and done with so quickly, yet she had been imprisoned for several weeks now. *At least it will all be over soon,* she thought. Death would be far better than having to live in a cold and damp cell only to have rats for company. As she lay down to sleep later than night, she heard the gentle patter of footsteps coming from the spiral staircase. Not the usual heavy clumping sound of a warden's steps but a sound that was softer, quieter. She assumed another woman had been accused of witchcraft and thought nothing of it. The steps became louder as they drew closer. A bunch of keys jangled and, shortly afterwards, her cell door was open. Raven, opening her eyes, looked down at the dirty floor and through the corner of her eye, caught sight of a pair of bright yellow shoes. Made of silk with small diamonds in the shape of a crown, they were exquisite and sparkled under the flame of the gaoler's torch.

A sumptuous yellow gown adorned with elaborate beading and jewels hung neatly over the shoes and as Raven raised her head, she realised Queen Elizabeth was standing in her cell.

"Do I dream?" she asked the Queen as she rose slowly to her feet.

"Tis no dream," the Queen replied. "If thou seek to live cometh with me and I shall thee free." The Queen studied Raven, her long black hair dirty and knotted, her face pale and sullen and she held out her hand. Raven took her hand and bowed. "Tis no need to curtsey," said the Queen. "We are but sisters." Tears filled Raven's eyes and flowed down her cheeks. The two childhood friends stood together united for a moment before the Queen said, "Cometh now. Tis no time for melancholy." She motioned over to her lady-in-waiting who stepped forward, placed a blanket around Raven's shoulders and wiped the hay from her feet before placing them in a pair of warm sheepskin boots. Raven left the cell with the Queen and stepped inside a waiting carriage with four horses. In the dead of night, the carriage dashed away from the prison.

The carriage headed for Fulham Palace, a large country house alongside the banks of the River Thames where the bishop of London lived. The Queen also stayed at Fulham Palace as a country retreat when she was able to have a break in her schedule from state matters. In the carriage, the Queen told Raven she had known she was conducting witchcraft since they were teenagers and was willing to overlook the matter. However, she had only just learned that the woman accused of murdering and maiming the Williams brothers was her childhood friend and she couldn't bear the thought of her companion, who had made her childhood so happy, being put to death.

The horses galloped through the country, finally arriving at Fulham Palace. Queen Elizabeth told Raven she must leave England if she wanted to live. "Go," said Elizabeth as she placed a small leather bag of coins in her hand. "Go and never return for thou will be hunted and I'll not be able to save thee."

"I thank you, Your Highness," cried Raven. Breaking from royal protocol, she threw her arms around Elizabeth and hugged her. "Farewell thee, sister." The women parted, Elizabeth headed into the courtyard of the palace along with her lady-in-waiting, while Raven disappeared into the unfamiliar forest.

Raven had hardly set foot outside London in her entire life so the prospect of leaving the country where she grew up was nothing short of frightening. *Where shall I go? What shall I do?* she wondered. Crossing the English Channel to France was not an option as her fear of water made this impossible so she walked aimlessly in the forest until tiredness and fatigue overwhelmed her. She sat under a big tree to rest and eventually fell asleep. Early the following morning, a thick frost hovered over the damp earth while birds in the trees chirped, squirrels darted under bushes looking for food and a blackbird perched itself on a nearby log that was covered with bright green moss. Cold and hungry, Raven wondered what to do. She pulled out the purse Queen Elizabeth had given her and realised the money would only last a week if she were to eat and pay for several nights' lodgings. It was the beginning of very bleak life for Raven. Lost in an unfamiliar forest, she had to find her way out before she perished and time was of the essence. Magic was essential to find her way out of the forest yet all of her potions were destroyed by the fire that engulfed her home.

However, her weekly visits to meet her witch friends had taught her something important, for she learnt how to cast spells using herbs and plants. In order for magic to work properly, the right combination of herbs and plants was essential so she set about looking for three particular ingredients: stinging nettle, corn mint and borage. She found the stinging nettle rather quickly and later found the corn mint near a small stream, but she couldn't find the borage anywhere. After a few hours of rummaging through the dense forest, she finally found it. Delicately plucking the prickly leaves from the stems she felt relieved that she had found her three ingredients. She returned to her tree, sat down and began plucking all the leaves from each of the stems and held them tightly in her hands. Rolling the leaves around the palms of her hands, she closed her eyes and began chanting.

> "This forest I have lost my way
> Guide thee a safe place to stay
> The tree where I sit I shall lay
> And when I wake shall know the way."

With her eyes still closed and clutching the herbs, Raven lay down, wrapped herself in her warm cloak and slept.

When she woke, she noticed something quite peculiar. The earth where she lay began moving ever so slightly. She sat up and looked onto the ground and felt the vibrating underneath become stronger until the whole tree began shaking. She quickly jumped to her feet to see the tree changing colour. The oak tree with its thick grey trunk began emitting all sorts of different colours. Blue, green, pink, red. All of the colours began merging and became brighter as each second passed. Raven felt as though the ground beneath her were about to give way so she grabbed hold of the tree to steady herself. Then it all stopped in an instant. The colours were gone, the earth stopped shaking and Raven found herself standing in front of the same oak tree. She thought the magic spell must have worked for she turned away from the tree and began walking in the opposite direction until she reached a clearing. She felt as though she knew the way out of the forest and kept walking until she reached a road where she heard a noise from the distance. It was an unfamiliar sound, like a loud rattle. It became louder and louder until a big rectangular object came hurling over the horizon. Coming towards Raven, the object became bigger and louder as it drew nearer. Frightened, Raven raised her hands and shielded her face, not knowing whether the loud object would attack her. Then the Volkswagen Kombi van roared past and kept going down the road until it faded out of sight. The year was 1980.

It took Raven several days to realise she had travelled through time. Upon seeing the Volkswagen for the first time, she retreated back into the forest and decided to walk alongside the road until she reached a town. What a shock it was to see hundreds of the same rectangular objects moving up and down the roads, many of them different sizes and colour. She thought it was rather odd that, out of all the different rectangular objects, all of the tyres were exactly the same. Although she didn't know the word for 'tyres' she referred to them as 'the black wheels', like the wheels of a carriage she was so used to seeing in the sixteenth century. She was fascinated at how quickly these vehicles moved and turned and the noises they made. Some vehicles were so long they could fit a family of seven or eight in them, with the children at the back facing out of the back window. The dirt tracks she was accustomed to were now concrete roads with lanes in each direction. Houses were made of brick with big glass windows instead of tiny little windows. Everything was big – houses, cars, buildings. Raven thought everyone in the town must be very rich due to the sheer size of everything, as she was used to living in a very small house in a poor village. Glass didn't even exist in Raven's time so walking past houses and seeing her reflection in the windows was simply unbelievable.

She kept to herself and made a little hut in the nearby forest using the bark off an old tree for a roof and gathered up kindling to light a fire. She hunted for rabbits and caught fish at a nearby stream. Most evenings, when darkness fell, she walked into the town, taking in all of the bright lights and moving cars, and she studied people walking up and down the streets. As much as it was overwhelming, it was also fascinating and Raven thought she might like to stay put for the time being. She felt safe as long as she stayed away from the general public. They were also strange, with all their colourful clothing. Women in their big frilly shirts and colourful slacks, their faces painted in different colours – blue eyeshadow, red cheeks and pink lipstick. Even the men wore brightly coloured suits with their sleeves rolled halfway up their arms and, like the women, their hair also tousled to form perfect waves and flicks around the sides, while the back was slightly longer, giving rise to a popular hairstyle called 'the mullet'.

One particular evening, Raven felt tired from walking around the town so she sat down for a rest and leaned back against a small brick fence outside a quaint little house. Her movement triggered the porch light and within a few seconds, the bright light lit up the front of the house. Not knowing what was happening, Raven quickly stood up and turned around. The front door opened and an older woman appeared on the porch. "Who's there?" the lady shouted. Raven stood still, frozen. She didn't know whether she should run or keep still. "Whose there?" said the voice again. A nearby dog began barking so the lady stepped off the porch and began walking towards the front gate. She stopped when she saw Raven standing there. Somewhat perplexed, the lady looked Raven up and down and noticed the dirt on her legs, her dishevelled hair and her bony arms. "Oh dear," she said. "Are you all right, my love?" Raven didn't answer. "Come inside and have something to eat." The lady put her arm around Raven and ushered her into the house where they both sat down on a big old sofa. "Where are you from?"

"I am lost," Raven answered quietly.

"Do you live here in town? Are you homeless?" she asked.

Raven didn't understand the phrases 'town' or 'homeless' but she deduced that the lady was asking where she came from. "My home. It is but ash," Raven answered.

"Ash," the lady muttered. "Hmm. Well my name is Betty Williams. Stay here and I'll go and make some tea, then we can have a proper chat."

A big cream rug covered most of the shiny wooden floorboards in the lounge. On the cream rug sat a large glass coffee table with a newspaper. The front page heading read *The Finlay Gazette*. Raven leaned over towards the newspaper when something caught her eye. She was unable to read most of the writing, however, she could clearly make out the date of the newspaper. Realising she was four hundred years into the future, things began falling into place. The cars, the houses, people walking the streets wearing strange clothing and speaking to each other in modern English. Sinking back into the sofa, Raven felt sick for she realised her magic hadn't worked in the way she had expected.

Betty returned with a pot of hot tea and a plate of sandwiches. Raven devoured the soft fluffy bread and the sweet tasting jam. It was delicious, she thought, as she finished the plate and drank her warm tea in a little white china cup. Betty asked all sorts of questions, none of which Raven could answer honestly so Betty assumed Raven had been in an accident and was suffering from amnesia.

"My poor dear," said Betty after realising that Raven spoke limited English. "You will stay with me until you begin to remember who you are."

"Oh, kind lady," said Raven. "I thank thee."

"Thee!" said Betty. "How odd a word. It's like you're from a different era. Well then, let's get you into the bathtub and into bed. It's getting late."

As Raven slipped into the hot steaming bath, the dirt from her body melted away and the rosy colour of her pale skin returned. Betty filled the bath with bubble bath and as Raven lay beneath the water with just her head poking out, she popped the bubbles with her fingers. Unsure of what to do with the shampoo bottle, she poured most of its contents in the bath and watched as the empty bottle floated on the surface of the water. Raven slept in a big double bed in the spare room and was amazed at the size of the bed. The curtains and bedspread were both painted with pink roses and it reminded her of her childhood with Elizabeth with the pink and red roses that filled the vast halls of the palace.

The next few years came and went and Raven spent much of those early years thinking how she could get back to the sixteenth century. She returned to the forest every week, searching for herbs in which to concoct a spell to return home. However, her best efforts were in vain for, over the years, the sprawling forest with its mossy logs, wild growing herbs and long grass was now, for the most part, a park with short grass, concrete paths and a children's play area. Raven realised that her old life was now well behind her and, as the years went by, she became more entrenched in the twentieth century. Life wasn't that bad though as she and Betty forged a close bond. They enjoyed baking together and visiting old shops, looking for old teacups. She loved watching television and as her English improved, Betty thought it would be in Raven's best interest to have her educated properly. Betty arranged daily tutoring for Raven to prepare her for the entry exam into the nearby grammar school. Raven worked hard and attained the results she needed to pass the English and Maths exams.

One afternoon she came running into the lounge room, shouting, "I did it! I did it!" She waved an empty envelope in one hand and a letter in the other. Betty almost stuck her knitting needle in her finger from all the excitement. Standing up, she gave Raven an enormous hug, her wrinkly hands patting Raven on the back.

"I knew you could do it," she said. "I'm so very proud of you."

Raven held Betty's hands, her beaming face flushed with joy. "Thank you for all you've done for me."

When Raven finished school she found herself a job in a nursing home where she learnt all about modern medicine. Gone were the old ways of making spells using weeds, plants and herbs. It was already prepared in tiny little bottles and tablets and the nursing home was filled with them. Hundreds of new medicines meant a whole new world of potions she could make. In her spare time she studied modern witchcraft and became an excellent potion maker. She tested minor spells on people she disliked, such as her boss, Matron Keely, a rather menacing older woman who consistently shouted at her staff. Matron felt that installing fear in her staff would mean they would work harder if they feared a telling off.

One evening, when Raven was about to finish her shift after a twelve hour day, Matron made her stay back and change all of the beds in the wards. Raven explained that she had to get home to prepare Betty's dinner who was now a very old lady. Matron didn't care and threatened to sack Raven if she disobeyed her orders. So Raven stayed back and however quickly she worked, it still took three hours to complete her jobs. When she finished and raced home, she found Betty lying on the kitchen floor. She had tried to prepare her own dinner and climbed up onto a stool to reach a can of beans and fell. Raven called the ambulance immediately but later that night Betty passed away from her injuries. Raven was furious, angry, inconsolable and vowed to seek revenge on Matron Keely. And that was that.

The following week in the staff tearoom, Matron sat down to eat her lunch. Marmite sandwiches and a cup of tea was the usual, however, on this particular day, her tea didn't seem to strain very well when she poured it from the little china pot. She removed the lid of the tea pot and peered inside. Nothing seemed out of the ordinary, except that some of the tea leaves stuck to the sides of the pot so she picked up her teaspoon and gave a little stir. "There," she said, placing the lid back and pouring a little milk into her cup. She then took a bite of her Marmite sandwich and another until she finished three whole sandwiches. She wiped her mouth on a paper napkin and picked up the little china cup, holding it very daintily with her thumb and index finger. Raising the cup slowly towards her mouth she smelled the fragrant aroma of the tea, the steam drifting up into the nostrils of her nose. She took a little sip, slurping it, then another.

Meanwhile, Raven sat close by, watching Matron drink every last drop of tea. Raven smiled as she watched Matron stand up, pop all of her dishes in the sink leave the room. Nothing out of the ordinary occurred that afternoon, however, all of the staff were aghast when the next morning, Matron called in sick. It was Matron's first sick day in over twenty years and her record that she was so proud of – not having had a day off in her whole working life – had been broken. Everyone, including the elderly residents, spent the day gossiping to one another as to what was wrong with Matron. They thought she must have been very, very sick. Even the doctors began talking about Matron's absence when she rang in sick for the second day in row. Raven continued about her work tending to patients, writing up their charts and assisting the doctors. Everything went on as usual for Raven except for the big smile she wore to work for every single day that Matron called in sick.

A week later, and to everyone's surprise, Matron turned up for work. She begrudgingly walked into the building with her head down trying her best to shield herself from everyone. She knew people were talking about her, for every time she passed the nurses their whispers would stop and they would quickly look away, pretending they were busy. Matron rushed to the staff room, stood in front of her locker and when she looked around all of the doctors and nurses having their morning tea gasped in horror. Matron's usual crimson cheeks were covered with big red scabs that went all the way up to her forehead and all the way down past her neck. A big puss-filled scab covered the tip of her nose. In the week she was absent from work, her hands had aged thirty years. They were wrinkly, veiny and her fingers had begun forming into little claws.

Her lush brown hair, which she wore in a tight bun every day, had turned grey and wiry and clumps of it stuck out of her bun. At the age of fifty, Matron now looked ninety. She scared the children who were visiting their grandparents and the adults didn't want her to come near them for fear of catching something. Within a month, Matron required the help of a walking stick as her bones had become so brittle. She lost so much of her vigour and energy that one morning she sat down in the lunch room for a rest and fell asleep, her head bent down to her chin, her arms dropping down her sides until her fingers almost touched the floor. As staff came, ate their lunch and went, Matron slept. In the afternoon, while several doctors sat together with their coffee and clipboards to discuss their patients, she slept. That night when the day staff had all gone home and the night staff arrived for their shift, she slept. When the cleaners began cleaning out the bins in the staff room, she slept. That was how Matron was thought of amongst her peers. She was a horrible person who made everyone's lives so miserable that nobody actually cared enough to wake her. They all relished the peace and quiet.

It was not until the following morning that somebody actually cared enough to see if she was all right. A junior doctor bent down and called her name. "Matron," he whispered. She did not wake so he called her name again. Worried, he touched her hand and when he gave her a little shake she slid down her chair and onto the floor. Her time to die had come early from the spell Raven had put in her tea. Now there would be nobody shouting down the halls at the nurses, there would be nobody standing at the reception desk every morning, ensuring that her staff were on time for their shifts. She was dead and Raven realised how easy it was to be a witch in the twentieth century. Nobody held Raven accountable for the Matron's death. She had gotten away with it and it was easy.

When Raven cast her spell on Griffin and James Williams, she felt that she was well within her right to do so. After all, they were bad men who stole, plundered and put fear into the village. However, with her newfound knowledge of modern medicine, she cast spells on anyone who crossed her even in the slightest way. One morning, she arrived at work with a ladder in her tights. Her new manager, who happened to be a lovely lady whom everyone respected, asked her to change them, even giving her a five-pound note to pop over to the supermarket across the road from the nursing home. Raven didn't like being told what to do, yet she did what she was told and walked across the road to the supermarket. She bought the new pair of tights. She changed into them. She did not stop there. When the new manager went home that evening, she ran a hot bath and undressed. When she pulled her tights off, her legs had turned a horrible dark purple colour. The purple began at the tips of her toes and went all the way up to her waist. Meanwhile, Raven sat at home in front of the television, thinking about her new manager trying desperately to scrub away her purple legs. Raven laughed as she stuffed a cream bun in her mouth. She thought her manager must be on route to the hospital by now. The next morning Raven's manager arrived at work in her blue uniform, her purple legs well and truly visible under the stark white tights. It was two weeks before the purple began to fade which meant a planned holiday in the Caribbean had to be cancelled.

All of this newfound magic gave Raven a sense of importance and she felt powerful for the first time in her life. Gone was the timid young girl born in the sixteenth century who was able to concoct a few spells. She had knowledge and realised that this knowledge would make her a force to be reckoned with if she took this back to the sixteenth century. Although she loved the twentieth century and all of the modern things that man had created, she thought that she could change the past. She wanted to go back and save her mother but realised doing so would mean that she might not be able to travel back to the twentieth century. The next day at work, she wondered, *what would I really miss? Nobody!* she deduced. *I would miss nobody, and nobody would miss me. Well, I would miss one thing, my cream buns. I would also miss my washing machine, microwave, a flushing toilet, hot showers every day, chocolate eclairs, gas fires to keep me warm at night, my hot water bottle, my beloved television on which I spend hours watching my favourite shows. Hmm.* Suddenly saving her mother's life didn't feel so important. However, she was aware of something that was very valuable. It was the most powerful thing on earth. More powerful than time travel, more powerful than anything man could ever create. There was only one problem. It was in the possession of her sister, her twin, who she was separated from at birth.

One Summer's day in June, a nervous Raven entered Bishops Park. The landscape had changed significantly since the sixteenth century. Although the oak tree was still in the same place, it was much bigger. It's trunk was dark and thick and several people could stand behind it and not be seen from the other side. Walking through the playground, children scooted around and played on slides while nervous mothers scooped up their little ones every time they fell over. Nannies sat together on benches, feeding babies while they chatted. It was a warm morning and everyone seemed happy. Raven held the gate open when a young mother had trouble trying to navigate her wide buggy through the narrow gate. After thanking Raven, the mother and her young children disappeared into the playground.

At the other side of the park, the entrance to Fulham Palace had an arch big enough for horses and carriages to enter into a quaint little courtyard where a fountain sat in the middle. The bishop's living quarters and a chapel were housed together at one side of the courtyard. The facade had been restored as the small open windows from the sixteenth century now had modern day glass panels. The paths leading to and around the palace had been laid in concrete so that tourists could walk around the grounds and enjoy all of the gardens. Wandering around the palace, Raven's thoughts turned to the night when Queen Elizabeth saved her life. Although it was over four hundred years ago, it felt like yesterday. Over the years, kings and queens had come and gone and man had changed a world in which people doubled their life expectancy with the help of modern medicine. Transport and machinery that arose from the Victorian period changed people's lives forever. The invention of the lightbulb meant that people could enjoy a longer day and the possibilities were endless with the invention of the jet plane and space travel. Life wasn't a miracle, it was man who was the miracle.

Raven found the oak tree, stood at its base, pulled out a small glass jar and sprinkled its contents over her hands. She gently placed her hands onto the tree, the rough surface of the trunk prickling her soft skin. Closing her eyes she whispered:

> "Here I return to find my home
> A long way gone have I to roam
> Take me back through the tree
> And when I wake home I shall be."

When Raven opened her eyes it was dark and deathly silent, with the exception of several birds chirping from a nearby tree. She looked up to a black sky and a full moon shining above the tops of the trees. Specks of light from the moon shone down on small patches of earth. It was just enough light for Raven to realise she had travelled through the tree for her clothes were different to the ones she wore when she entered the park. Breathing a sigh of relief, she looked down and noticed the blue skirt hanging down to her ankles where brown slippers covered her little feet. A white blouse with puffy sleeves and little silver hooks pulled the front together, tied up in a little bow. An apron sat neatly around her waist which was tied at the back. "So," Raven muttered, "I am a peasant. We shall have to change that." She walked briskly through the forest. She wasn't used to the darkness. There were no street lights, no headlights from cars and buses, just small shadows on patches of grass from the moon. Feeling relieved when she saw Fulham Palace in the distance, she knew she was safe. However, on closer inspection, something looked out of place. The gardens were completely different with newly planted shrubs and flowers. *Oh dear!* she thought. *Something is not right.*

"Who goes there?" came a voice from the other side of the garden. Not knowing what to do, Raven ducked down and hid behind a bush and kept silent. Again, the voice said, "WHO GOES THERE? Speak or the dogs will seek you out."

"It is I, a girl," said Raven, her voice quivering. "I mean no harm."

"Show yourself." Raven slowly stood up and a man holding a lantern above his head began walking towards her. "I am Bishop Terrick. What business do you have on my property?"

"Bishop Terrick?" replied Raven. "You are not Bishop Grindal?"

"Grindal?" quipped the bishop. "Are you a mad woman?"

Seeing the confusion on Raven's face, the bishop invited her inside the house. He was intrigued that she thought the current bishop of London was someone who had actually died in 1583. He wanted to know where she came from and who she was. After all, it was a rather strange occurrence to find a woman hiding behind a shrub on somebody's property late at night.

Inside the house, the bishop removed his cloak and handed it to a young servant who hung it on a row of pegs next to the front door. Raven nervously followed the bishop into the warm drawing room and he motioned her to a sofa where the same young servant poured a cup of tea from a grand looking silver teapot. The room was dimly lit. Candles and lanterns sat on side tables scattered around the vast room. A fire in a large marble fireplace crackled and hissed when another servant placed several logs on top of the dwindling flames. Settling on a large red velvet chair opposite Raven, the bishop pulled out a pipe from his pocket and tapped the ashes onto a small china dish. "I wonder if the lady has a name by which she calls herself."

"Gudrun, sir." She dared not tell the bishop she called herself Raven for fear of being found out that she was a witch. And she knew first-hand what happened to witches.

"Well then, Gudrun. Let me formerly introduce myself. I am Richard Terrick, Bishop of London, as appointed by our good prime minister, the Duke of Devonshire."

"Devonshire? Did you say Devonshire?"

Bishop Terrick studied Raven in a rather perplexed way. "Yes. Our prime minister, *the* Duke of Devonshire."

It dawned on Raven that she had not returned to 1563 for she hadn't even heard the term 'prime minister' let alone the Duke of Devonshire. Growing up in the young Princess Elizabeth's court, she was familiar with the names of the men on the Privy Council, as well as the Queen's trusted advisors, and none of them were named Devonshire.

Raven was too afraid to offer any further information. She didn't want to ask the bishop what year it was for fear of being accused of having gone mad, a condition that would almost certainly see her being locked away, perhaps forever, as she had no family that could help her.

"Well, Gudrun" said the bishop, lighting his cigar. "I am rather curious as to why you seem to think that I am Bishop Grindal when he has been dead for almost two hundred years." As the bemused bishop waited for an answer, he sipped on a small glass of brandy.

"I must have fallen on my way home which led to the confusion." Raven was satisfied with her answer, as she had half expected the old man to ring for the servants and throw her out of the house. Yet he didn't so she just assumed he believed her.

"In which borough of London do you live?"

Raven realised that each sip of her tea gave her a few seconds to think of an answer before she spoke.

"Fulham, sir."

"Ah, then." The bishop raised his eyebrows. "We are neighbours."

Raven finished drinking her tea. She felt uncomfortable in the presence of a man of the clergy and wanted to get as far away from the bishop, the house, the palace, as possible. She needed to be inconspicuous, to remain under the radar and stay away from people in order to avoid anyone finding out who she really was. Perhaps, she thought to herself, she could cast a spell on the bishop to make him sleep so she could make her escape. No, that wouldn't work, she thought, for she did not have the right potions. "Thank you for the tea, sir," she said. "Now I must be on my way."

"On your way?" chuckled the bishop. "Why, you don't even know where you are. No, I cannot let you leave in your confused state. You will spend the night and I will send for your parents in the morning." Standing up, the bishop went on. "My servant will escort you to the guest bedroom. Good night, Gudrun."

The bishop was gone and Raven remained seated while the young servant, who was standing at the door, spoke in a soft voice. "This way, ma'am."

On the way to her room, Raven glanced at a newspaper on a table in the hallway. It was titled *The London Evening Post* and, to her astonishment, the date read 21 June 1765. Raven had arrived in eighteenth century London, otherwise known as the 'Georgian period'. King George III was on the throne and London was now a bustling and lively city in which to live.

Raven stayed at the bishop's house in Fulham Palace for the next few weeks. The bishop tried in vain to find her parents but, of course, he was never going to find them and Raven kept up the pretense of having amnesia so that she didn't have to explain who she really was. At the bishop's house she had a warm bed to sleep in and cooked meals every day. She ate vegetables and fruits that were grown and picked from the garden to accompany dishes of wild boar, hog and chicken. She read books and particularly loved reading *Robinson Crusoe* by Daniel Defoe. She read poetry by Jonathan Swift and enjoyed taking walks and picking flowers in the vast gardens of Fulham Palace. During her walks, Raven used every opportunity to return to the oak tree where she tried to find her way back to 1563, however, none of her magic worked. She had used up most of her potions and by the time every last drop of potion was gone, she had cast spells on almost every tree in Bishops Park in order to get back home. Each spell created a different blueprint on the trees and as Raven didn't know the correct spells, it was uncertain which trees were magic and where they actually took you was anyone's guess.

Raven's frequent visits into the forest piqued the bishop's interest. He wondered why she wandered off so often, after all, why would she possibly need to spend so much time in a patch of land that was muddy, dense with trees, cold and solitary. So, one evening when the bishop and Raven were playing a card game called whist, he thought it a good opportunity to challenge Raven on her frequent trips into the forest. A quick witted Raven informed the bishop that she was fascinated with all of the herbs and plant life that was not immediately available in the palace gardens. Raven now felt at ease with the bishop, with whom she had gotten on very well over the past few weeks, that she showed a total lack of judgement and went on to say that she remembered her father was a doctor and used herbs when he couldn't find a cure for a particular illness. Perhaps it was the strength of the single glass of brandy she drank that evening, but the lie she told the bishop was ultimately her undoing.

The next day when Raven was still sleeping in her warm bed, the bishop sent a letter to a several friends in high places who had access to all sorts of medical registers, one being the Company of Surgeons. The reply that was returned to the bishop was done in person by a doctor named William Cheselden, an outstanding doctor who was the first warden of the Company of Surgeons. He felt the need to deliver his report in person as the letter contained some very grave findings. So the two men met for lunch and Doctor Cheselden duly informed the bishop that there was no doctor in the whole of England that Raven had named on that fateful evening. This worried the bishop on an immeasurable scale as he couldn't believe that someone he helped would deliberately lie to him. This prompted him to follow Raven so he could see for himself what she was really up to in the forest. And so one sunny afternoon when Raven assumed the bishop was having a little nap in his chair after lunch, as he often did, she slid out the back door and set off down the little path and through the gardens and into the forest.

The bishop was indeed sitting in his chair after lunch but he was only pretending to sleep. When he opened one eye and looked out the window he saw Raven strolling through the garden towards the forest. Very carefully he followed Raven, keeping a good distance so she couldn't hear or see him. Deep into the forest, the bishop witnessed with his own eyes Raven rummaging around the foliage, collecting herbs then mixing and crushing the herbs into little jars she produced from her cape. As she began chanting, with her hands held up against tree after tree, the bishop had seen enough. Realising she was a witch, he hurriedly made his way back and ordered his staff to lock every door and close every window. However, Raven never returned to the house as the bishop and his staff had expected. Nor did she return to Fulham Palace. She never even made it out of the forest, for her spell had finally worked. She did indeed travel, but not back to 1563.

PART 3 - 2019

CHAPTER 28

A bleary-eyed William opened his eyes, stretched his arms out wide and yawned. Jumping out of his big bed, he rummaged around his bedroom, found his favourite pair of jeans crumpled up into a heap on the floor and quickly got dressed. Outside his bedroom was the grand staircase. He casually walked down all twenty-five steps and through the entrance hall where an antique table stood with dozens of lilies in a vase two feet high. When he walked into the kitchen, Mother and Isabel were already eating breakfast.

"Ah, there you are! We thought you wouldn't be up for hours," said Mother. As usual, she was sitting next to Isabel, drinking her morning coffee. The table was filled with pastries, scrambled eggs, fresh fruit and toast.

"What time did you get in?" enquired Isabel as she buttered a slice of toast.

"About three," replied William. "Everyone decided to stay at the party but I didn't feel like it."

"What a night," said Isabel, yawning.

William and his family had been out celebrating as he had just finished his fourth year of medicine. He had worked very hard and earned top marks.

"Looks delicious," said William as he sat at the head of the table. "I'm starving."

"So, what's the plan for today, guys?" Mother sipped her coffee.

"I have a free day," replied Isabel. "Shall we go shopping and spend the day together?"

"I have to pop into the office for an hour but after that I'm free. Sounds great. And you, Will?"

"I'm catching up with some of the guys from class later on."

"Look at my boy, all grown up," said Mother, smiling proudly. "And joining the workforce soon. Seems like last week you were still playing with your cars in our old house."

"Yep," replied William. "Who would have thought I'd actually be called 'Doctor' one day."

"Which hospital are you doing your rounds in?" asked Isabel.

"St. Bart's. Found out yesterday I'm under the supervision of Dr Edwards."

"Dr Edwards! Do you mean *the* Brian Edwards?"

"Yes, Mum. *The* Brian Edwards, Dad's best friend."

"Oh, how lovely. I'm sure he'll take good care of you. I must pop over and say hello one day."

After Dad's name was mentioned, there was silence at the table until breakfast was finished.

"Well then," quipped Mother, "I'm off now. Isabel, I'll call you a bit later and we'll meet somewhere for lunch and shopping."

"All right, Mum."

When Isabel and William heard the front door slam shut, William turned to Isabel. "So tell me. How's Dad?"

"He's really good, Will."

"Is he happy? What's he been doing?"

"He's as happy as can be expected. He's still helping the poor and needy. He has his own house now. It's small but really nice."

William felt a little sad at the prospect of not being able to see his father very often once he began his final years at university. Knowing how hard his father worked, he knew that being a doctor meant very long hours. He wouldn't be able to travel through the oak tree for long periods of time, just a couple of days here and there. Isabel, on the other hand, travelled back to see her father every few weeks as she was about to begin her gap year before attending university.

"Isn't it strange how things work out?" pondered Isabel.

"What do you mean?"

"Well, you and I, our lives, our future. Had it not been for that stamped envelope we wouldn't have gone to university, we wouldn't be living in this lovely big house and Mum would still be working day and night to support us. I think it's marvellous what you did."

"Thanks, sis." William winked at his proud sister.

When William travelled back home after George had died, he found the envelope that Mrs Maguire had given him in Bristol. Not knowing what to do with it, he kept it for safe keeping as it contained her address in Surry and William thought maybe one day he might check in on her. So he placed the envelope in a shoebox at the bottom of his wardrobe. It remained there for a whole year and he had completely forgotten all about it. However, one afternoon, as he opened his wardrobe, the top shelf fell down and with it came a bunch of clothes, a hockey stick, a small stack of old school books and several notepads. He realised he needed to clear out his wardrobe as the hockey stick landed on his head and he acquired a nice looking bump, a purplish-blue in colour, that didn't begin to subside for almost two weeks. It hurt too! *Well that's it*, he thought. *I just can't keep stuffing everything into my wardrobe anymore.* So he decided to clear it out. Out came everything, including an envelope, which fluttered down landing gently on the floor. When he picked up the envelope and turned it over something caught his eye. The little black stamp with a picture of Queen Victoria might be worth something to a collector. He thought it was lucky that the stamp hadn't gone through the postal system which would have deemed it worthless. So one afternoon he set off for the Royal Philatelic Society in London where he had it valued.

As it happened, this particular stamp was considered extremely rare in the twenty-first century and William sold it for a fortune. The money that William acquired from the sale of the stamp paid for his and Isabel's university fees and he bought the family a grand house which meant Mother didn't have to work two jobs. She became the director or nursing at the local hospital. It was a job she loved because she was able to spend every night at home with her children.

The stamp was sold to an anonymous buyer on the strict instruction that the stamp remain on the envelope. Although William never knew who bought the stamp, the buyer was Edward Smythe, who was a distant relative of little Maisie. After

Mrs Maguire moved to Surry with her children, she was given the opportunity to buy the merchandise from the store where she worked after the owner retired. She jumped at the opportunity and leased a bigger store in which to sell the goods. She became very successful and the expansion of railway lines into London meant thousands of people could travel into London every day so she leased another store in the heart of London. Within a year she had expanded her store to include imports from overseas, from Mongolian cashmere to unusual items from Africa. Her store was unique and her idea for British people to be able to buy overseas goods meant that she became very wealthy. Her idea was born out of her seemingly insignificant visit to the Great Exhibition with David, back in the Summer of 1851. By the time she passed away, she owned one of London's biggest department stores and her children of Dormitory A and their dependents amassed a large fortune. Edward Smythe was a collector of old and rare things and when he came across the penny black stamp, with Mrs Maguire's handwriting on the envelope, he just had to have such a special family heirloom.

"Well then," said William as he finished eating his croissant, "today's the day."

"Are you ready?" asked Isabel.

"We have to find her. We can't let mum know she actually still exists."

"I know. We can't let it rest until it's done."

"You're right Izzy, she's just too powerful with it. Who knows what she's capable of?"

"All right then," said Isabel, "what's your plan?"

"I'll start at Greenwich where she grew up. It's a long shot but worth a try."

"Please come home safely," begged Isabel.

William returned to his bedroom and got ready for his next journey through the oak tree. He left the family home and headed for Bishops Park. He passed the site where the caretaker's house used to be. Several years ago, Simon Brown left the house early one morning and never returned. He left all of his possessions in the house and it was thought by the locals that he ran away from something, or someone. The old house was so dilapidated that the council pulled it down and the site became a grassy area that blended in with the rest of the park.

Returning to Bishops Park once again, William felt that awful feeling, the anxiousness and the heaviness in the pit of his stomach at the fear of the unknown in what lay ahead. The oak tree soon came into view and before William placed his hands upon the mammoth trunk he, looked up and contemplated its thick brown trunk and its branches covered in thousands of pretty green leaves at the very top that gently swayed back and forth in the wind. Then, all of a sudden, thick dark clouds enveloped the sky. The bright sunny morning became dark and a gusty wind quickly picked up and blew the trees, ferociously blowing branches hither and tither, making loud crackling sounds as they broke away from the tree.

William's mop of brown hair blew wildly in his face. He stood back from the tree and turned around towards Windermere Road. His old house was still there, which seemed quite normal, yet none of the trees in the street were blowing to and fro. They were still, calm, serene. Suddenly a strange feeling came over him. He felt goosebumps all over his arms and he felt as though he was being watched.

Looking around the park, he noticed a shadow in the distance standing next to the elm tree. He thought the shadow looked like a woman for her long dark hair was also blowing furiously in the wind. Then all of a sudden the wind stopped blowing and the park regained its composure. Every tree in the park stood still as if they were surrendering to the woman who appeared to hold some kind of power over them. A deathly silence ensued and William's heart began pounding. He stood there silently, wondering whether he should turn around and run for his life or stay and find out who the woman was. She hadn't realised William was watching her and when she turned around, a bright sparkle from her neck glistened. William held his breath for he recognised the gold circular disc. It was the amulet that Raven stole from David six years ago. The amulet was tied to a leather strap around the neck of Raven, for she had returned. As soon as William recognised the witch, he took a few steps backward and fell over. He sat there, unable to move from sheer terror.

"William," whispered a voice. He turned around but nobody was there so he assumed he was thinking things, that his mind was playing tricks on him. After all, he just had the shock of his life seeing Raven in Bishops Park so he deduced that anything was possible. "William" came the voice again. He didn't recognise the voice so he quickly stood up and found the courage to start walking over to the tree where Raven was standing.

"Right!" he said to himself. "This is ridiculous, I'm hearing voices of people who aren't there. I am not going to be frightened by anything or anyone." As he continued walking towards the tree, a second shadow emerged. "Mother?" William stammered.

Startled, Mother emerged from behind the tree. "Yes, it's me," she answered. "You weren't supposed to be here."

"What are you doing here, Mum?" William asked. "What's *she* doing here?" He pointed to Raven.

Raven began laughing. "Oh, you silly boy. You thought your mother was good, didn't you? Well she's not. She's just like me."

"I know she has powers like you because you are sisters," replied William. "But, Mum, what is going on?"

"You weren't supposed to be here, you weren't supposed to see me!" Mother repeated.

"What are you talking about?"

"The amulet!" cried Mother. "Your father gave it to Raven six years ago, you were there!"

"I remember," said William. "She killed George, her own son!"

"The amulet doesn't work unless both Raven and I are present because we are twins. Here!" she said, turning over the amulet on Raven's neck. A small inscription read:

"A jewel of gold
the passage of time
in two hands
doth break the line"

"These hands!" Mother continued. "This means both our hands. Raven can't be immortal unless we both place our hands upon the amulet and read the inscription at the same time."

Raven interjected, "She's right. We are over four hundred years old but we will live forever as long as we have the amulet."

"Why are you helping her, Mum? She's evil."

"Go home," said Mother sternly.

"I won't leave until you tell me why you're helping her."

"I can't tell you. Just leave."

Before William could say another word, Raven and Mother stood behind the tree, placed their hands on the amulet and began chanting, "A jewel of gold, the passage of time, in two hands doth break the line." Over and over again they chanted those words.

William scurried around the tree and they were gone. "Mum!" he shouted. "Come back!"

William had an awful feeling he would never see her again. He dreaded going home to tell Isabel what happened in the park. How could he break it to her? What would he say? What would *she* say?

William ran from the park in utter shock. Mother and Raven opened their eyes, their hands still clutching the amulet. They were still in Bishops Park. Raven knew something had gone terribly wrong. Her hands were old and wrinkled and her hair had turned white. She changed from a beautiful woman to an old lady in a matter of seconds. Mother, on the other hand, had not aged at all. As soon as Raven saw Mother, she pulled the amulet from her hands and shouted, "What have you done?" Tugging at her ragged grey hair, she burst into tears. "Look at me!" she roared. "I'm old!"

"Yes you are," replied Mother. "You need the talisman."

"What? A second stone? What is this talisman you speak of?"

The talisman was the most precious stone on earth. While the amulet bestowed eternal life, the talisman bestowed eternal youth and has healing powers beyond any medicine known to man. This particular talisman was called the 'Morning Star'. Shaped like a star, it has a small ruby stone at every one of its five points. Around the perimeter an inscription read, '*In perpetuum this stone, two stones eternal youth*'.

"Where is this stone?" shouted Raven. "I must have it!"

"I can't tell you. It will be too powerful in your hands."

"You know where it is?"

"Yes," replied Mother. "It's in the possession of Drys. Only he can reverse the ageing of your skin, your hair and your body, but I need it too. You see, I need the powers of both stones to complete my own mission."

"Your mission? Are we not on a mission together? Was that not our plan? To live forever? What has happened to you, sister?"

"I want the Morning Star just as much as you and I, too, will stop at nothing to have it."

"Well then, sister. It seems we have a problem."

The sisters stood there, staring at each other. Both knew what the other was thinking. They had to find Drys. The question was, who would find him first.

CHAPTER 29

In the year 1540, on the outskirts of Hastings, was a small village of three hundred people. Most of the villagers were farmers, some were merchants, but they were all happy and formidable. They looked out for one another. When crops were at risk during summer droughts, the villagers took turns working day and night to water them. Mothers looked after one another's children and an annual party was held every Christmas at the church to celebrate life and give thanks to one another. The people of the village didn't have much in so far as money or possessions but they had their families and each other and that was all they really needed. The main street consisted of a small cobbled road with a few small shops and at the edge of the village lived a blacksmith. He mainly kept to himself and chose not to participate in any annual festive activities whatsoever. In fact, nobody really knew anything about him. He hardly ventured out of his house, except to the store for food and the local dairy for milk.

The blacksmith was a young man and very strong, which was quite odd considering he was actually five hundred years old. He was so old that he was privy to the great Battle of Hastings in 1066. When the battle ended, England had a new king, William the Conqueror. It was during the battle that the blacksmith found the talisman in a saddlebag on the King's horse. Thinking he might be able to sell it to buy a new pair of shoes or a warm sheepskin for winter, he tucked it away safely in his pocket. All was well until the next full moon, when strange things began to occur. The old man, with his hunchback and crippled fingers, went to sleep and when he woke the hunch on his back began to disappear. He was now able to stand upright. His shoulders were broad. His crippled fingers stretched out and his wrinkly skin became taught and smooth. Over the next hundred days, he had transformed from an old man to a fit, athletic, handsome younger version of himself. His head was covered with lustrous wavy black hair which hung below his chiseled chin.

The young man called Drys settled in Hastings and because of his strength and physical abilities, it wasn't long before he caught the eye of England's new king. On Christmas Day in 1066 when, William was crowned King of England, he noticed Drys amongst the crowd of revellers rejoicing in the celebrations. The King thought Drys could prove useful in his court and invited him to work alongside him as protector of the realm. Drys was delighted at such a prestigious offer and the very next day, left his home for the King's palace in London.

Life was perfect for Drys. His strength and power grew as each year went by. However, the King's courtiers began gossiping when, after ten years of his peers ageing, Drys looked exactly the same. After twenty years, the King's advisors were seriously concerned as they thought some kind of witch was living amongst them. They were especially concerned for the King who was growing old and nearing the end of his reign. Fearing he may be hanged for witchcraft, Drys left the palace in the dead of night, never to return.

For the next five hundred years, Drys spent his time settling in villages around England. The blacksmith moved every twenty years from village to village. He became so paranoid of people finding out his secret that he completely retreated from all human contact. In a small village in South East England, now known as Kent, Drys settled in a small farmhouse and built a shed to work in so that he didn't have to walk into the village every day. If anyone needed tools made they would come to him. The furnace in his shed kept him warm in the winter where he slept on a small bed.

One morning, he was woken early by the sound of his horse neighing. He quickly jumped out of bed, lit a small lamp and, holding it up as he peered outside the shed, saw a dark shadow moving towards him. "Who goes there?" he shouted. There was no answer and the shadow disappeared so Drys thought it was a wild animal and returned to his warm bed. The following day, the village was abuzz with activity for a newcomer had arrived which was such an unusual occurrence. Children milled around this newcomer while their suspicious and protective mothers pulled them away. The village elders sat on their porches, rocking their chairs to and fro, as they watched the newcomer walk slowly past them. They watched as the newcomer stopped in the middle of the dirt road and made eye contact with a farmer who happened to be walking past.

"Excuse me, sir."

"Can I help ye?" asked the farmer.

"I am looking for Drys."

"The blacksmith?" said the farmer, feeling somewhat perplexed. He wondered why anyone from out of town would be looking for a recluse who kept to himself. "He lives down yonder, just over the small bridge. First on left."

"Thanking you kindly."

"Well then," said the farmer, looking the newcomer up and down, "you look tired. Have you travelled far?"

"Yes. Very far. I am old and tired. I shall be on my way now."

"I am Gembert," said the farmer. "You are welcome in our village."

"And I am Raven."

In his shed, the blacksmith clanked his hammer, shaping various tools and weapons for farming and hunting. What began as a bright and sunny morning very quickly turned dark and cloudy. It began to rain heavily and lightning lit up the sky while angry thunder clouds crashed together. The blacksmith put down his tools and stood outside in the pouring rain. He had never seen such a ferocious sky. Realising his clothes were completely wet and his hair soaked, he ventured back into the shed and almost jumped right out of his skin when he saw Raven standing in front of the fire.

"Who are you? What is your business?" Drys demanded as he watched the old lady hobble around the small room and perch herself on a chair in front of the fireplace.

"Hello," said Raven, her voice crackling. "I hope you don't mind if I sit. As you can see, I'm very old and tire easily."

"What do you want?" he asked nervously, although he knew exactly why Raven was in his house.

"I want the talisman. And *you* have it. You see, I have the amulet which has granted me eternal life but, as you can see, I need the talisman for eternal youth."

"No. I will not hand it over. They are too powerful together. Nobody can have both."

"Give it to me," Raven said softly as she held out her wrinkly crooked fingers. "Or I will cut you down. I may be old but I can still cast spells. I can blind you with my words. I can maim you with my hands."

"No you will not!" yelled another voice. Both Raven and Drys spun around to see where the voice was coming from. It was Mother, standing at the front door.

"Ah," said Raven, smirking. "You found me."

"I have spent what feels like a lifetime looking for you and Drys. I am here to collect what is rightfully mine."

"I don't think so," said Raven, laughing.

Turning to Drys, Mother held out her hand. "Please. I need the talisman. For the sake of my family, please give it to me."

"No!" Raven stood up, threw her arms up in the air and began chanting, "Cut them down, to the ground, show me the talisman." Over and over again she chanted while Drys and Mother stood still, unable to move their legs from her spell.

"What is happening?" screamed Mother. "I can't move! I can't feel my legs."

Drys grabbed hold of a table and tried with all the strength in his body to move his feet but it was no use. Raven's spell was too powerful. All of a sudden, a shimmer of light appeared from within the cracks of the floorboards. The blinding light got brighter and brighter until the whole house completely lit up.

"There!" shouted Raven. "It's under the house!" She scurried on all fours, scraping at the floorboards, trying to pull them up with her bare hands. She found a small hole in one of the floorboards and grabbed it, pulling up an entire row of crumbling wood. Then she stopped, puffing and out of breath. Right beneath her, lying on a small box under the house, lay the talisman. Before she took another breath from her shrivelled up lungs, she lurched down and grabbed it. Clutching it, she raised it up and brought it close to her face. The small stone was mesmerising. It was as if she was in a trace. "It's mine! Mine! Mine!" she shrieked. "Now I am *the* most powerful being on the earth. I shall live forever! I will be beautiful again and you will both shrivel up and die!" Drys and Mother were helpless, still unable to move.

Raven pulled out the amulet and locked it together with the talisman. Twisting the stones together, it was a perfect fit. She waited for her face to return to its natural beauty and her body to become slender and smooth but nothing happened. She looked over at Drys who was muttering something under his breath. He was casting his own spell, for he was still more powerful than Raven. His legs began to twitch, his feet began to move, and within a few seconds he was standing over Raven. He was furious, his face red with rage. He pulled the stones out of Raven's grasp and held it over her head.

"No!" she yelled. "Let me live. We can own the stones together. We can rule the earth together." She was desperately hanging on to what pathetic life she had left.

"You will be aged another hundred years and die on the next full moon."

"Please!" begged Raven. "Let me live!"

"Leave now or you will die an even worse death than this."

Raven slowly stood up, sobbing and whimpering and headed for the front door. She turned around and begged for her life one last time. Without another word, the door opened wide and Raven hung her head and walked through it. The door slammed shut. She was gone.

Drys turned to Mother and held out his hand. "I've been waiting for you."

"I don't understand," replied Mother.

"When I found the talisman there was a small parchment tied to it. It was in French and said the rightful owner's familial bonds would be broken forever without it." Drys took Mother's arm and lay the stones in the palm of her hand. "Go and use these stones for their true purpose. I have been living for too long. I am tired of moving. I am tired and want to grow old as nature intended."

Mother clutched the stones close to her chest and closed her eyes. The tears rolled down her cheeks.

***

As the sun began to fade over Bishops Park on a cool winter's evening, Mother stood outside the front door of her home. She had returned safely through one of the oldest trees in Bishops Park. Her heart was pounding so hard it felt like it might jump right out of her chest. She felt so nervous that her hands began shaking, yet she was smiling. The person standing next to her took her hand and squeezed it gently. "It's okay," he whispered. "Everything will be all right." She squeezed back. "Are you ready?" he asked.

"I'm ready."

Mother slowly turned the door handle and opened the front door. Standing in the hallway were her beloved children, Isabel and William. They were waiting for her along with another very special person who was standing right beside Mother. It was their father. Together, the talisman and amulet had the power to return David to his family and it was Mother who brought her husband home. For the first time in ten years, the Pritchards were together again and nothing was going to change that. Isabel and William felt happy and relieved knowing they would never have to travel within the trees again. How wrong they were, for the amulet held a very dark secret. It wasn't the end for the Pritchard's journey, it was just the beginning.

THE END

Lightning Source UK Ltd.
Milton Keynes UK
UKHW011001271221
396222UK00001B/351